the VENGEANCE

a novel set in Buddha's times

SUBHASHIS DAS

olive turtle

NIYOGI BOOKS

Published by
NIYOGI BOOKS
Block D, Building No. 77,
Okhla Industrial Area, Phase-I,
New Delhi-110 020, INDIA
Tel: 91-11-26816301, 26818960
Email: niyogibooks@gmail.com
Website: www.niyogibooksindia.com

Editor: Sukanya Sur
Cover design: Kaushikee
Layout: Shashi Bhushan Prasad
Cover images: one AND only/shutterstock; zef art/shutterstock

ISBN: 978-93-89136-28-9
Publication: 2019

Printed at: Niyogi Offset Pvt. Ltd., New Delhi, India

... at the lotus feet of the
Enlightened One

Overcome the angry by non-anger; overcome the wicked by goodness; overcome the miser by generosity; overcome the liar by truth.

—The Buddha

Contents

PROLOGUE

According to the Buddhist Pali canons, ancient India, between sixth and fourth century BC, was divided into sixteen *mahajanapadas* or great kingdoms such as Kosala, Magadha, Gandhara, Anga, and others. Kosala's capital Savathi (this version of the city's name used in the book is in Pali, while in Sanskrit it is Shravasti) was the seat of kings like Mahakosala, Pasenadi (this version of his name used in the book is in Pali, while in Sanskrit he is Prasenajit), and Vidudabha (this version of his name used in the book is in Pali, while in Sanskrit he is Virudhaka or Virudhaba), who belonged to the Ikshvaku race. The vihara (monastery) Jetavana, adjacent to Savathi and one of the finest in those days, was created for the Buddha and his *sangha*. The Buddha had spent around twenty-five monsoons in the tranquil environment of Jetavana, where both here and in Savathi, he is known to have performed many miracles. Pasenadi and his wife Mallika converted to Buddhism, but much akin to the kings of the rest of the *mahajanapadas*, Pasenadi too ruled in accordance with Vedic norms.

Alongside these kingdoms were *ganasanghas* or *ganarajyas* (republics), as that of Kapilavatthu (this version of the city's name used in the book is in Pali, while in Sanskrit it is Kapilavastu), Koligrama, Kusinara, Pava, Veshali, and others that may have manifested from chiefdoms or from earlier times (Thapar 2002:

146). Though the clans that ruled the *ganasanghas* held themselves as Kshatriyas, they did not quite pursue the Vedic varna system, nor observed Vedic rites, but worshipped at 'sacred enclosures and groves' (Thapar 2002: 148). These people observed non-Vedic tribal customs and even practised endogamy, 'a custom abhorred by all good Hindus' (Allen 2010: 4).

The Sakyas, according to several scholars, could have been more of the Mongoloid hillmen type, 'akin to the Tibetans' (Smith 1958: 74). It could be that their name 'Sakya' may have had its origin in *saku* or *sal* (*Shorea robusta*) trees, held sacred by all in those times. The more intrepid researchers, however, establishes a relationship of these Sakyas with the Scythians of Central Asia, who too were known as Sakyas (Attwood 2012: 47–69).

The Sakya state of Kapilavatthu was a *ganasangha* in the foothills of the Himalayan range. The river Rohini was accepted as the border between the countries Sakya and Kolia. Despite its real name Mahanagara, the capital was also known as Kapilavatthu. It was in this *ganarajya* that Gautama had grown up prior to his becoming the Buddha. Chieftains of Kapilavatthu, Suddhodana and Mahanama, were regarded as rajas or nayakas.

Rajagaha (this version of the city's name used in the book is in Pali, while in Sanskrit it is Rajgir or Rajagriha), also known as Kusagrapura and Girivraj, was the capital of Magadha kingdom established by Maharaja Bimbisara of Haryanka dynasty. He married Kosala Devi, the sister of Maharaja Pasenadi. The Buddha and his disciples, while in Rajagaha, generally resided in the cave of the Gijjhakuta Pahad (this version of the hill's name used in the book is in Pali, while in Sanskrit it is called Griddhakuta) or the Vulture Peak Hill. However, as Rajagaha was associated with both Mahavira and Buddha, Bimbisara adored both these ascetics.

Although the tale of Vidudabha has many disparities among the various Buddhist texts across the world, the focal story remains unchanged. Though Vidudabha and his mother Vasabhakhatiya are believed to be wicked by some, Vidudabha is held sacred in a few Buddhist nations, and in Japan he is even venerated as a deity. Reading his vindictive feats in the ancient texts, one may tend to despise him; but in this book I have rendered Vidudabha as a compassionate and a benevolent person who is insulted, abused, and ostracized by his father, Maharaja Pasenadi of Kosala, his grandfather Nayaka Mahanama of Kapilavatthu, and the Sakyas for no fault of his own. Their condescending attitude towards him and his mother Vasabhakhatiya transforms this unassuming youngster into a vindictive person, yearning to avenge them all. While Buddha wanders, preaching his dhamma of love, peace, and compassion across a wide stretch of land in East India, including the kingdom of Kosala, he fails to make an impression on the agitated and spiteful mind of Vidudabha, who indulges in the utmost vicious deed of slaughtering Mahanama and annihilating Kapilavatthu and the Buddha's very own people, the Sakyas.

Although disputed, Sagarwa lake, locally known as Lambu Sagar (long lake), is accepted by a section of scholars and archaeologists to be the spot where the carnage of the Sakyas was possibly committed. This instance of such a large-scale massacre was very rare in ancient India. There does not even seem to be an agreement on the number of mass executions of the Sakyas. Hiuen Tsang, also known as Xuanzang, was a Chinese Buddhist monk and translator who travelled to India in the seventh century. He put the number of deaths to around 99,900,000, while a few other scholars estimate this figure to be about 9,990.

Although the book is based on facts, a few fictitious incidents have been woven into the narrative to arouse curiosity among the readers, while several events have been left out for brevity. The book does not intend to offend any individual or community.

Endnotes

Allen, C. 2008. *The Buddha and Dr Fuhrer: An Archaeological Scandal*. London: Haus Publishing.

Attwood, J. 2012. 'Possible Iranian Origins for the Śākyas and Aspects of Buddhism'. *Journal of the Oxford Centre for Buddhist Studies*, vol. 3.

Smith, V. 1920. *The Oxford History of India: From the Earliest Times to the End of 1911*. UK: The Clarendon, Oxford University Press.

Thapar, R. 2002. *The Penguin History of Early India: From the Origins to AD 1300*. New Delhi: Penguin Books.

BOOK I

Savathi and Kapilavatthu

Give even if you only have a little.

—Dhammapada

In the park close to the river Achiravati, the palace gardener's young daughter Mallika, who was in her early teens, would play with her friends all through the morning. Come afternoon, they would return home for lunch. Many a time, the children's mothers would pack small *thailas* of snacks, which they would share amongst themselves at play.

One fine summer morning, when the children played *chua-chui*, a few bald monks walked across the park; the sound of their steps soft as breeze. Mallika stopped her game as she gaped at them. She had seen the same band of wandering ascetics many times earlier, and each time she was filled with an indescribable fascination. She had, of course, seen different kinds of ascetics: the naked *acelas*, the *niganthas*, the *ajivikas*, and also the messy and the unkempt-haired and long-bearded sadhus. Although these *bhikkhus*, also known as *parivajijakas*, begged like other monks, they looked different to Mallika as they were bald, did not grow beards, and donned orange-coloured, flowing robes. She further observed that their countenances, particularly of the one who led the procession, had a calm contentment that enticed her towards them.

Mallika suddenly ran after them, calling at the top of her voice. The *bhikkhus* stopped and turned around to see a young girl darting towards them. The older one looked at her with a smile. Coming close to him, she panted and looked straight into his eyes. Then suddenly, she placed her satchel of rice gruel, which was her midday snack, into his begging bowl, little realizing that she had offered alms to the Great Renunciator, the Sakyamuni Buddha. He blessed Mallika for her act of selfless compassion who, having no understanding of the event, fled to resume the game with her friends.

Afterwards, the Buddha turned towards his *sangha* and uttered, '*Ananda ayam kumarika imesam kummasapindanam phalena ajjeva kosalaranno aggamahesi bhavissati*' (This girl today will be the chief queen of the kingdom of Kosala through the fruits of this portion of the gruel). Ananda, the Sakyamuni's cousin, and one of his closest disciples, responded, 'But Master, she is ugly, deformed, and has a very unappealing appearance. She is unfit to be a queen.'

'May be, my dear Ananda,' replied Tathagata. 'But for her selfless *kamma*, she will attain this elevated position. It is with the right effort and right action that one gets the right result.'

Shortly after the departure of the *bhikkhus*, an exhausted man trudged slowly through the park. He was Pasenadi, the king of Kosala. Defeated in war and abandoned by his army, Pasenadi was returning to his palace in Savathi. Unable to move any further due to hunger, thirst, and exasperation, he dropped on the ground, unconscious. When he came to his senses, he found his head placed on a young girl's lap, whose name he soon learnt was Mallika. In the cool shade of a dense *simul* tree, the girl softly ran her fingers through his long hair, comforting his weary body and disconsolate mind. As Pasenadi opened his eyes, she offered him water in a small sal leaf cup; the cool water satiated his thirst in the oppressive heat. After a modest natter with one another, Pasenadi softly confided that her kind gesture had won his heart. Lying on her lap, he declared that he was the king of Kosala and would love to have her as his queen. Mallika warily disclosed that she was the daughter of a *malakar*, the king's gardener, and was unworthy to be a queen.

'I do not care for that, my sparrow,' uttered Maharaja Pasenadi, slowly yet very resolutely. Bringing his lips very close to Mallika's, the king firmly said, 'I will marry you and make you my queen this very day.'

Pasenadi called on the palace *malakar*, the father of Mallika, and expressed his desire to tie the knot with his daughter. The *malakar* and his wife, having no words to express their disbelief and glee, readily consented. Late in the afternoon, Mallika was summoned by Pano, the king's old aunt, and she was carried with much splendour and honour to the palace. That night, she was wedded with Maharaja Pasenadi and subsequently anointed the Maharani of Kosala. The citizens of Savathi, looking at their new queen, remarked, *'Āvuso, mallikā devī buddhānaṃ tayo kummāsapiṇḍe datvā tesaṃ phalena taṃ divasaññeva abhisekaṃ pattā, aho buddhānaṃ mahāguṇatā ti'* (That is Queen Mallika who gave alms to the Buddha).

Everything changes as everything is impermanent.

—Sutta Pitaka

'It's a girl.'

The midwife, jutting her head out through the slightly opened door, announced with a broad smile to the waiting group of impatient women. Jeeva, the palace messenger, who stood at a distance in anticipation, inquired, 'Is she healthy?'

'Yes, yes, she indeed is. Go and inform the king,' the midwife replied.

'How is the queen?'

'She too is fine.'

Jeeva rushed through the inner corridors to the king's court where Pasenadi, the king of Kosala, sat in his assembly. The happy news was conveyed to the king through his minister. Pasenadi sat on his royal seat sombrely. Hearing the news, he emitted an unenthusiastic trifling smile; as his first issue, he had expected a son as his successor.

The news that Kosala has been blessed with a princess spread like wildfire across the capital of Savathi. The court's functioning, too, had to be stalled for the day.

Later in the day, the king slowly walked into the *atur ghar*, the room where Maharani Mallika and the newborn would be kept for the next twenty-one days. No males were permitted to enter the quarantined room except Pasenadi's widowed aunts, Mallika's mother, a few other womenfolk of the palace, and, of course, the king himself.

Seeing the king, his old aunt Pano, the widowed sister of his late father, lamented in her hoarse and blaring voice, 'My dear Pasu, it is indeed heartbreaking to have a girl and not a boy as your first child.' Pasenadi shook his head and signalled her to keep quiet as the queen was asleep. He walked towards her and stood by the bed, gazing at his newborn daughter. He ran his fingers through the queen's hair and she gradually opened her eyes, delighted to find the king standing by her.

'Maharaj,' Mallika softly uttered, 'when did you come?'

'Just now,' replied the king.

'Your Majesty, forgive me for giving you a daughter instead of a son.'

'Needn't worry, Maharani. Perhaps, the next time it will be a boy,' Pasenadi expressed an unrestrained optimism.

The king took the little princess in his arms and kissed her forehead. Looking at his newborn daughter for a while, he returned her to the women attendants.

'She is very sweet,' said Pasenadi.

'Are you happy, Maharaj?' inquired a very concerned Mallika.

'Certainly, I am. But I would desire a yuvraj of Kosala as my next issue,' said Pasenadi, a slight trace of dissatisfaction clear on his face. 'Now you sleep, my queen, as I have matters of the state to attend,' saying this, the king slowly walked out.

Savathi soon turned into a festive town, as the royal announcers drummed their *dafali*s to proclaim the birth of the kingdom's princess. However, the old folk across the town brooded, 'As the first child, a male heir to the king would have been better...'

The news of the newborn princess was dispatched to the father of Mallika, the palace gardener, and to Pasenadi's brother-in-law, Maharaja Bimbisara of Magadha, and his wife Maharani Kosala Devi, the sister of Pasenadi. Messages were sent across the *mahajanapadas* of Anga, Panchala, Gandhara, Kamboja, Surasena, Vatsa, and Chedi, and to the various *ganarajyas* of Malla, Shakya, Koliya, Licchavi, Vrijji, and others.

The citizens of Savathi, like in other parts of the country, had various religious beliefs. A number of them followed the ritualistic sacrificial tantra, while a few practised Charvakism. Vedic Brahmanism was pursued austerely by a multitude, while several others observed the animistic form of the tribal faith. Akin to other regions of the land, most people of Savathi deserted their earlier religious practices and were fast embracing the doctrines of the *samanas*—fatalism of Makkhali, *avihimsa* of Mahavira, and the *dhamma* of Buddha. Pasenadi, however, had already converted to Buddhism before his marriage to Mallika. She called to mind how, prior to her marriage, while playing in the park near the river, she used to be piously attracted towards the Buddha, knowing nothing about him at that time. Now, subsequent to her marriage to Pasenadi, she too adopted his *dhamma*.

The arrival of monsoons in North India brought with it the Buddha and his *sangha* at Jethavana, enthusing delight in the hearts of both the king and the queen, as well as among a large number of the citizens in Savathi. Hearing of the Buddha's arrival at Jethavana, the king summoned his minister and expressed his desire to visit Tathagata in the afternoon and seek his blessings.

It's not easy to maintain seclusion, not easy to enjoy being alone. The forests, as it were, plunder the mind of a monk who has not attained concentration.

—Bhaya Bhereva Sutta

They waited; Pasenadi and his men.

They waited outside Gandhakuti, a *kuti* (hut) created for the Buddha in Jethavana. But the wait was to be long as the Buddha and his *bhikkhus* were deep in their *vipassana*. For Pasenadi, this wait was like a pilgrimage. He was here to see the Master and convey to him the news of his daughter's birth. Maharani Mallika, having given birth to the princess that day, was not in a position to accompany her husband to the Enlightened One.

The wait had the king wander into thoughts of the past.

Pasenadi reminisced about Buddha's narration of the incident when Mallika had given away her food to him and the *sangha* while playing in the park. It made him realize that she indeed was a benign and an empathetic woman, a quality rare among the contemporary younger generation. Pasenadi also recalled that it was the same day she had nursed him, and he married her the same evening. Mallika greatly revered the Buddha and that pleased Pasenadi even more. Despite her uninviting looks, Mallika's quick wits enabled her to win a significant position in the kingdom. Pasenadi, finding her diplomatic frame of mind useful, discussed matters of the state with her as much as he would do with his ministers and advisors.

Maharaja Pasenadi was nearly of the same age as that of the Buddha, yet he venerated the Sakyamuni the most. Although

Pasenadi was drawn towards The Awakened One prior to his marriage to Mallika, he recalled that he did not always have such adoration for the Buddha. Pasenadi's memory took him back to his younger days when he was a yuvraj. He had returned after the completion of his education in Takshashila, when he had run into Gautama in his palace for the first time. Gautama had been invited there as the guest of honour of Pasenadi's father Mahakosala, the then king of Kosala. Both being in their early thirties, Pasenadi couldn't believe that Siddhartha was an ascetic who, at this age, had renounced the world in search of truth. Pasenadi, in reality, hadn't witnessed a holy man till now who was young, soft-spoken, calm, happy, and so content. Besides, Siddhartha was bald, grew no dishevelled beard or moustache, and donned only a robe.

Understanding the prince's dilemma, Siddhartha helped him clear his ambiguity, 'Age is of the body, O Yuvraj.' So striking was his voice that Pasenadi couldn't move his eyes from him. 'Strange are the ways of the world. A soldier, no matter how young, would fight to kill and defend his own land. A venomous snake, no matter how small, could kill or attempt to do so, as a small fire can cause a big damage. In the same manner, O Prince, a young *bhikkhu* too can renounce the world in search of the eternal truth.' Pasenadi remembered how he had reflected on Siddhartha's words of wisdom the entire day, which created a great impact on him.

By the time Pasenadi became the king of Kosala, Gautama had attained enlightenment and was transformed into the Buddha, hence the name. Pasenadi learnt that 'Tathagata' was one name among various others that the Buddha was christened with, the name meaning 'the one who has arrived' (*pahuncha hua* in Hindi, a term used to describe a spiritual or a sharp-witted person).

So influenced were Maharaja Pasenadi and Maharani Mallika with the Sakyamuni that they literally worshipped the ground he walked on and would regularly invite him and his *sangha* to the palace whenever they would be in the country. Eventually, at Jethavana, in the outskirts of Kosala, a monastery was constructed for the Buddha and his *bhikkhus* where they would conduct their *vipassana*, apart from taking shelter from the rain. Although both Maharaja Pasenadi and Maharani Mallika had converted to the *dhamma* of the Buddha, their admiration and tolerance towards other faiths were no less praiseworthy.

***

Maharaja Pasenadi sat on the grass for long, waiting for the Buddha to emerge from Gandhakuti. He gazed at the forest that surrounded Jethavana, where the songs of the birds and the calls of the peacocks resounded. Peace was omnipresent. This must delight the Buddha, he thought, little knowing that for The Awakened One peace was not an external state but an inner condition of being in which he was. Untouched by the outer surroundings, he was in union with his innermost existence and the world outside had no influence on him whatsoever.

The overcast monsoon sky was increasingly turning dark, with threatening rain clouds hovering above. Restlessness gradually seized Pasenadi, for he had been waiting too long for the Buddha now. His thoughts coasted to his brother-in-law Bimbisara, the king of Magadha, who, although enthused by the teachings of Vardhamana of the Licchavis, was also inspired by the acute dedication of Gautama as a *bhikkhu* to attain the truth.

Pasenadi recollected that when the news of Siddhartha's enlightenment in the village of Uruvela reached Bimbisara in Rajagaha, he had the shrubs of the bamboo forest at Venuvana cleared for Gautama, as he often rested and bathed in the pool there prior to his *bodhihood*. Venuvana was converted into a fine-looking park which Bimbisara wished to gift to Tathagata. The maharaja arrived at Jethian near Uruvela, where he aspired to join the 17 km trek from Jethian to Venuvana in Rajagaha with the Buddha, his followers, and hundreds of other people.

Pasenadi's train of thoughts was interrupted when he heard footsteps inside Gandhakuti. The resplendent figure of the Buddha emerged gracefully from the hut. Pasenadi and his men lay prostrate on the ground where The Blessed One stood, and they all kissed his feet in deep reverence. He raised his palms, bestowing blessings and reassurance from fear to all.

The root of suffering is attachment.

—Sunakkhatta Sutta

'Maharaj, I hear that you have been blessed with a baby girl?' the Sakyamuni asked Pasenadi, embracing him.

'Yes, Master,' Pasenadi replied humbly, folding his two palms together. 'I, however, had expected a prince.'

'O King, many women are known to be wiser than men. You needn't worry, as your daughter too could grow up to be one such wise woman,' the Buddha said, raising his right palm to reassure the king.

'Master, I beg you to come to my palace tomorrow and bless both my child and Maharani Mallika,' requested Pasenadi, with both his palms clasped.

'I shall,' the Buddha replied smilingly. 'But you seem to have become stouter since the last time we met, O King.'

'You too have noticed. How do I control this, O Master?'

'You have an insatiable appetite, Maharaj, which is definitely a big obstacle in the path of *dhamma*.'

Pasenadi seemed annoyed with the Buddha's analysis, but remained silent.

'Such obesity comes from gluttony,' continued Tathagata. 'Greed is a bad *kamma* and it needs to be curtailed, or else it will bring bad results for your health. To live life in the Middle Path is the best way; neither much food nor less is desirable, as more food will tell on your health and less food will weaken you. Therefore, Maharaj, have only that much that satisfies your hunger. It will surely help in reducing your plumpness.' Tathagata's left palm was raised, facing his heart, while with his right, he formed a circle by touching the tip of his thumb and index finger. Then he raised his right palm towards the king, both as a blessing and to show *abhayadana*. 'I shall have to bid you goodbye for now, O King. It is time for us to set out on our *pindapata*,' saying this, Tathagata smiled and lowered his palms. The offerings which Pasenadi had brought along with him were delivered to the *bhikkhus* of the *sangha*, and after kissing Tathagata's feet with deep veneration, the royal party departed.

The Buddha and his disciples trudged slowly towards the town, carrying their begging bowls. Pasenadi observed that even the walk of the *bhikkhus* exhibited calmness and contentment. He felt that watching their strides too was a sacred act that brought peace to his heart.

Digha Karayana, the senapati of the Kosala army, was also observing the monks. He turned to the king and asked, 'Maharaj, we gave them so much that it may last a month. So what was the necessity for them to go begging for food?'

Pasenadi smiled as they rode back on their horses to Savathi. 'Senapati, begging is not merely for alms. In fact, their begging is different from other beggars'. In their rounds of *pindapata*, they do not distinguish between rich and poor homes. On coming upon a doorstep, they call for the lady of the house to announce their arrival, but they never demand for food. They accept anything that is offered into their begging bowls. Neither do they refuse anything, nor are they selective while accepting something. Much is involved in this act. This is also a form of *vipassana* and it helps to do away with their favouritism and ego.'

***

The *bhikkhus* entered the town. Several passers-by bowed with profound reverence before them. Very soon, they were standing in front of a house where Moggallana called, '*Bhikkha dehi*, Mai.'

The door was flung open and a young woman emerged with red swollen eyes, probably due to incessant weeping. Looking at the Buddha's serene face, she threw herself at his feet, crying, 'Baba, help me. Please help me. My son died a few days ago. This grief and sorrow is unbearable ... give me strength to bear the loss, O Master,' the woman drenched his feet with her tears.

'Please get up,' Buddha helped her rise to her feet and consoled her. 'O Mother, losing a son is indeed a great agony. I can understand the misery you are going through. This is a twinge of pain that you alone have to go through, for no one can share it.' He brushed his fingers through her hair that comforted her, bringing more tears to her eyes. Gradually, she stopped sobbing and meekly said, 'I shall get some rice for you, O Blessed One.'

'Mother, in the normal course of events, we accept all types of alms as we do not distinguish the food offered to us. However, today we shall deny food from your house as a death has occurred here,' replied the Buddha. 'We can only accept rice if you can bring it from some other household.'

'Alright, Master, in that case I shall bring it from my neighbour. Please wait for a while,' the woman replied. She was about to leave in a hurry for her neighbour's place when the Buddha stopped her.

'Mother, get it if you so wish, but take note that no death must have occurred in the household from where you intend to bring the rice for us.'

'But ... ' saying this, the woman stopped immediately, realizing what the Master was hinting at. Then, clasping her hands before

The Venerated One, she spoke with tears brimming in her eyes, 'Master, O Master, thank you. I understand now ... '

'Mother, we are all attached to one another on this earth and to things that are dear to us. Everyone who is born will die someday and everything that has a beginning will end one day. All of us are attached to someone who will depart from this earth at one point of time, and we fall into *dukkha* when we are unable to bear the pain of their loss. Therefore, our attachment is the cause of all our sufferings. Like every mother, you too are strongly attached to your son. You could not accept his sudden death and it brought an immeasurable sorrow to you. But the death of your son is not an exclusive event, for there is no family on this earth where death has not occurred or shall not occur in the future.'

'Your elucidation, O Blessed One, is so true; it has brought me respite from my suffering,' the woman bowed down and kissed the Buddha's feet.

'And now, Mother, forgive me for having tried to make you understand the harsh reality of the world in an unkind way, but would you now kindly offer food in our begging bowls from your house?' Buddha asked the mother smilingly.

You only lose what you cling to.

—Dhammapada

The newborn was named Vajira by Pasenadi's aunt Pano. She went on to become the king's loving pet. Whenever indoors, he would spend his time playing with his little girl. Unlike her mother, Vajira was fair and good-looking. Years rolled on and Vajira, in due course, evolved into a graceful girl. Meanwhile, Kosala still remained deprived of a prince with Mallika demonstrating no inkling of being pregnant.

'Wonder why I am not conceiving,' Maharani Mallika expressed her deep anguish to Maharaja Pasenadi one fine morning.

'Well, if you feel that something is amiss, let me send for the *vaidya* for your check-up,' said Pasenadi. He instructed the *rajvaidya* to examine the queen. The royal *vaidya* made a comprehensive examination of the maharani and soon after reported to the king on her state of health.

'Yes, Your Majesty, something is indeed wrong with Maharani's health that I am unable to detect. May be, we can call for Jivaka,' reported the *vaidya*.

'Alright then. Jivaka is indeed the most famous *vaidya* of the land. Where would Jivaka be now?' the maharaja turned to his minister.

'My Lord, I have learnt that he is now in Rajagaha, he being the personal *vaidya* of our own Maharaj Bimbisara of Magadha,' replied Sudatta, the prime minister.

'Fine, summon him immediately.'

Jivaka Komārabhacca was born in Rajagaha to an unknown father and a courtesan mother named Salavati. After growing up, he travelled to the University of Takshashila to study medicine for seven long years. Post the completion of his study, he returned to Rajagaha where he was granted the status of the *rajvaidya* of Magadha as he had cured Maharaja Bimbisara of a fistula. He settled in Amravan (mango orchard) in Rajagaha. Here, Bimbisara commissioned Jivaka's residence as well as his hospital so that he could even provide care for the Sakyamuni Buddha. Very soon, he became the most eminent of all *vaidya*s.

Jivaka arrived at the beckon of Pasenadi. He scrutinized Maharani Mallika for a few days and subsequently recounted her condition to the king.

'Maharaj, I have observed and examined Maharani Mallika intensely. It is a matter of great misfortune. If you permit me, My Lord, I would enlighten you about it.'

'Please speak, *rajvaidya* of Magadha. Do not hold back anything even if it is appalling,' the king pleaded Jivaka.

'Maharaj, the Maharani can no longer bear a child.'

'What! Why is that?' the king expressed in utter dismay.

'The Queen shall not be able to conceive any more as her problem lies in her *bacchadani*. I have no cure for this,' Jivaka soberly informed Maharaja Pasenadi, letting him down.

***

Being a person of strong individuality and a firm attitude, Maharani Mallika stood apart from the rest of the women of her era and region. However, a gradual transformation started manifesting in her behaviour as she turned into a conceited and an impolite person. Constant squabbles with her husband transpired with each passing day, and eventually both ceased to talk to one another.

One morning, when Maharaja Pasenadi was in his assembly, the courtier pronounced the arrival of the Buddha and his disciples.

'The court is dismissed for now,' announced the minister Sudatta. 'Tathagata is arriving here.'

Pasenadi and his people all rushed out to receive the Buddha. A mere glimpse of The Awakened One in the distance after almost a year brought much solace to Pasenadi's wounded heart. The entire assembly of Savathi went out to receive the Buddha and his *sangha*. The king lay prostrate on the ground and kissed the Buddha's feet. Subsequently, all took turns to kiss the feet of Tathagata and the rest of the *bhikkhus*. Raising his right palm, The Enlightened One offered blessings and *abhayadan*.

'Welcome to Savathi, O Great Master,' said Maharaja Pasenadi, clasping his palms.

Tathagata grasped Pasenadi's hands in utter delight and asked him, 'Maharaj, how are you, your family, and your subjects?

'We all are fine, Master,' Pasenadi spoke submissively.

The Buddha and his disciples were courted into the inner quarters of the palace. The *bhikkhus* sat on the floor in the *padmasana* posture.

'Where is the Queen, O King of Kosala?' inquired the Buddha.

'O Compassionate One, Maharani Mallika isn't the same as she used to be. We do not converse any more. Her supreme ego and high-handedness prevent her from talking to me,' replied Pasenadi.

'This, Maharaj, is not good for either of you. You forget that both of you are the guardians of the *mahajanapada* of Kosala.

Therefore, your personal fights will harm the kingdom,' the Buddha responded tenderly, yet quite resolutely.

'Master, her vanity makes it difficult for me to communicate with her.'

'But my dear Pasenadi, apparently you are only looking at her boastfulness, not at her compassion and her devotion towards you, towards the holy people, and even towards the state. Can you also not see how people revere her?' Pausing for a while, the Buddha continued, 'You must try searching for the reason that caused the sudden change in her behaviour. Thereafter, make truce with one another so that your bickering does not distress your people.'

'Yes, My Lord,' saying this, Pasenadi bowed respectfully to the Buddha.

***

With time, Mallika's superciliousness augmented and she quarrelled with her husband at the slightest annoyance. Pasenadi chose not to counter her with squabbles. With much fortitude, he remained considerate towards her. Months rolled by. On one bitter winter night, Pasenadi found Mallika to be extremely humble; she confided in him that despite taking all the medicines prescribed by the *vaidyas*, performing all the rites authored by the Brahmins, and giving in to the *totkas* of the female *bhaktins*, pregnancy still evaded her.

'Maharaj, should the throne of Kosala remain vacant?' inquired Mallika, suddenly bursting into torrents of tears, something which Pasenadi was absolutely unprepared for. His constant persuasion and consolation had no effect on the maharani's outburst. Her weeping sustained for a prolonged period. Finally fatigued, she gradually fell into a deep slumber.

Early in the morning, Pasenadi found the maharani to be a changed person, like she used to be. The arrogance and haughtiness in her eyes and face had disappeared. Looking at her husband, Mallika flaunted a broad smile. She stooped low on her reclining husband and planted a kiss on his temple, while moving her fingers through his hair.

This transformation in Mallika surprised Pasenadi. Remembering Buddha's advice, Pasenadi chose to seek the cause for the sudden change in Mallika's temperament. Later that day, the king called for his advisors to discuss about the entire episode of the queen. He asked them to decipher the reason for the strange behaviour of the queen all this time until today. He conveyed to them that perhaps her persistent shedding of tears the previous night had something to do with her reformation.

The advisors heard the king in deep contemplation and consequently discussed the matter amongst themselves.

After their protracted analysis, one of the elderly advisors spoke, 'Maharaj, this behaviour of the queen may seem strange, but is surely not extraordinary. That the queen was unable to be impregnated despite her various attempts is the prime cause for her behavioural variations. She was in torment that resulted from the deep guilt for not being able to produce the yuvraj of Kosala. Therefore, an insensitive and snobbish behaviour steadily crept into her as a defence against the world that she faced every day and which she thought was abusing her, or perhaps holding her guilty for not being able to give birth to a prince. May be, the elderly womenfolk of your family were taunting her for this. Inadvertently, she defended herself by creating a shield of superiority and ego against this guilt, which gradually turned her into a distressed person, ready to jump into a quarrel anytime. Following this, she underwent severe remorse. Your unwavering compassionate behaviour towards her led to her emotional outburst last night. She felt penitent and became the same old person once again. Your Highness, this, we feel, is what that must have happened with her.'

That evening when the king walked into his room, Maharani Mallika came to him and spoke very tenderly, 'Maharaj, I sincerely desire that you marry again, this time to someone who would bear Kosala the next king.'

Dhamma is the permanent, changeless truth of reality. It is immortal, and it confers immortality (the deathless).

—Patika Sutta

It was night-time in the kingdom of Savathi.

Both Maharaja Pasenadi and the minister Sudatta sat in the *sabhakuti*, the conference room, while Vadana, the secret informant, stood facing the two. The conference room was made soundproof by the Yavana builders using ingenious techniques, so that even a loud bellow indoors was inaudible outside the room, while the tiniest clink outdoor was clearly perceptible inside, making it an ideal venue for all the secret meetings of the state.

Sudatta signalled Vadana to commence with the information he had collected from his spies in Kosala and Savathi. Vadana fell silent. 'Speak without fear,' Pasenadi ordered.

'Maharaj, the people are worried that the Maharani has not yet given birth to a yuvraj.'

'Where are these gossips transpiring?' enquired the minister.

'In *sarai*s, marketplaces, wrestling *akhada*s, at weddings, on streets ... you name it,' replied Vadana.

Maharaja Pasenadi fell silent for a while to introspect. Then he signalled his minister to let the informant leave.

'Depart for now,' gestured Sudatta to Vadana, who, bowing both to the king and the minister, left the room.

'Sudatta,' Pasenadi spoke in a vexed tone, 'tomorrow before the court sits, summon the *rajjyotishi*. I have a matter of significance to discuss with him. Ask him to bring both the Maharani's and the Maharaj's horoscopes.'

'Yes, My Lord,' bowed the minister. The meeting was over.

Next morning, the royal astrologer had already arrived when Maharaja Pasenadi entered his assembly.

'Maharaj, the *rajjyotishi* is here with the horoscopes you sought,' Sudatta said. Pasenadi signalled the chief astrologer to come forward.

'*Rajjyotishi*, examine both the Queen and my horoscopes accurately and notify me about the birth of our next child,' the king instructed. The astrologer, nodding to the king, began mulling over the horoscopes.

After examining the *pothi*s for a long time, the *rajjyotishi* said, 'Maharaj, I have profoundly studied the horoscopes, both yours and the Queen's. The finding indeed is depressing.'

'Speak up, *rajjyotishi*. You have been our family astrologer since the time of my grandfather. Do not hesitate even if the news is disheartening,' the king beseeched the astrologer.

'The Queen's horoscope says about some problems in her *bacchadani* for which she can never give birth to another child,' disclosed the *rajjyotishi*. Gulping for a moment, the astrologer resumed, 'The horoscope further confirms that there is no remedy for this ailment.'

'What then could be a possible solution?'

'Examining your horoscope, Your Highness, I found that Kosala's future king would come from your next marriage.'

'Are you sure of this?' the king enquired.

'Maharaj, as sure there are stars and the sun in the sky. My readings, as Your Majesty knows, are etched in stone.' After a brief moment of silence, Pasenadi gestured the *rajjyotishi* to leave.

Lifting his head, Pasenadi gazed at the decorated ceiling of the assembly. A thought drifted into his troubled mind. Since he venerated Tathagata the most, if he could get to marry a Sakya princess he could cement this relationship with the Buddha's people permanently.

Little did Maharaja Pasenadi know that the Sakyas, who had begun to regard themselves as Kshatriyas, snubbed the Kosalas and their king, even though it was widely believed that the genealogy of Pasenadi could be traced to Lord Rama of the Ikshwaku Dynasty. Ignorant of such a bigoted opinion, Pasenadi felt that a marriage bond with a Sakya princess would bring him closer to the Buddha.

All we are is the result of what we have thought.

—Dhammapada

The winter was harsh that year. Most of the winter, the terai region of Kapilavatthu, the capital of the Sakyas, remained enveloped with a thick fog. But on that morning, there wasn't a trace of haze, and the glorious sun beamed blissfully on Kapilavatthu. A timid little mountain stream flew by an old and a sprawling banyan tree, emanating a lyrical sound. A bare-bodied old man was engaged in his morning yoga on an earthen platform below the banyan. He was Mahanama, the raja or the nayaka of the *ganarajya* of Kapilavatthu. Icy winds blew from the distant Himalayas despite the bright sunlight, but this hardly affected the elderly man.

Five aged men slowly lumbered towards the old man practising yoga. Coming near the tree, they squatted on the grass waiting for the old man to conclude his routine regimen, while they discussed some subject of substance in a hushed voice.

'What is the matter? Why are you all here?' Their conversation was interrupted by the voice of the old man who, after concluding his drill, was putting on his robe.

'*Johar*, Mahanama.'

'*Johar*,' said the old man. 'What is it that you could not wait till my arrival at the *santhagara*?'

'Honourable Raja, it is about a message from Maharaj Pasenadi of Kosala, which the *sangha* needs to address in urgency.'

'And what message is this?'

'Maharaj Pasenadi and Maharani Mallika of Kosala are devout followers of our Tathagata. In order to strengthen Kosala's relationship with Kapilavatthu, Maharaj Pasenadi seeks for the hand of one of our princesses in his second marriage.'

'How is that even remotely possible!' exclaimed Mahanama. He was about to speak further, but restrained himself. 'Let us meet in the *santhagara* around noon to discuss this matter.'

Mahanama, despite being an old man, had an upright posture and a healthy physique due to his regular yoga practice. No one could speculate his age correctly. He loved walking by the stream that flowed across Kapilavatthu. Mahanama had become the successive raja of Kapilavatthu after Sudhodhan's demise to find the *ganarajya*'s economy in the doldrums. Much was needed to perk up the condition of their army as well. Little by little, Kapilavatthu began regaining its lost status to become a strong *ganarajya* under Mahanama, as it had been during his predecessor's early years.

Lost in thoughts, Mahanama paced on the streets of Kapilavatthu as the townspeople greeted him. He soon arrived at a moderate-sized, bricked house and called, 'Vasu, are you home?'

A strikingly beautiful young woman appeared, responding to the call. She was Vasabhakhatiya, the daughter of Nagamunda and Mahanama. Seeing her father at the door, Vasabhakhatiya rushed out to touch his feet.

'Blessings, my child. Where is your mother?' the raja enquired.

An ageing, dark-complexioned woman emerged from indoors and touched Mahanama's feet. The old raja was led to a chowki in the first room. 'I shall not sit for long today,' Mahanama said hastily. 'I have much work to do at the sabha.'

'Will you not have breakfast, Master?' asked Naga, or Nagamunda to be precise. The Mundas were a tribe who had arrived in the terai region from the south-west of Kapilavatthu, much before the coming of the Sakyas in this country. Similar to the Mundas, the Sakya tribe revered the *saku* or the sal tree, considered sacred by both the groups. The Sakyas gradually embraced the Aryan way of life, while also retaining much of their original tribal characteristics. The Munda tribe had already begun moving away towards the east and the south of Kapilavatthu, but the Sakyas in due course of time had enslaved several Mundas of the region. Among the numerous enslaved was Nagamunda, who was Mahanama's *dasi*. The pretty girl Vasabhakhatiya was their love child. Being one of Mahanama's slave women, nobody dared to disrespect her, but they scoffed behind both Nagamunda and her daughter's backs.

'No,' replied Mahanama. 'You know that I do not eat without a bath and my morning rites. By the way, Naga, have you thought of Vasu's marriage?'

'Yes, but as her father, I thought you too would be worried about it,' replied Nagamunda gently.

'Shut up,' Mahanama suddenly flared up. 'I have many *dasis* from whom I have several children. Would that mean that I will keep worrying about all of their marriages?' Nagamunda and Vasabhakhatiya stood still, listening to the irate words of the old man. Composing himself after a while, he said, 'Alright, I have a plan for Vasu's marriage. If everything goes well, she will be married to a king and become a queen.' Both the women observed that a faint smile had appeared on Mahanama's lips.

Mahanama's pronouncement left both the mother and the girl stunned, but they did not dare ask him the name of the king to whom Vasabhakhatiya would be married.

'Soon you shall hear more about this good news,' saying this, Mahanama walked out of the house, closing the door behind him.

From attachment arises sorrow; from attachment arises fear. From desire arises sorrow, from desire arises fear. From craving arises sorrow; from craving arises fear.

—Dhammapada

The *santhagara*, meant for holding the conferences of the parishad or the council of the *ganarajya* of Kapilavatthu, was a brick-and-timber structure with thatched roof and a floor cleaned with cow dung and water. Mahanama sat on a raised dais, while the *amalas* or the councillors were seated on mats on the floor. As the meeting of the council was underway in the *santhagara*, an uneasiness was visibly reflected on everyone's face.

'I cannot have my daughter marry Pasenadi,' said a very fretful Mahanama. 'You all know that we Sakyas descend from a superior origin and can never imagine to marry a Kosalan. In that case, how can I give my daughter's hand in marriage to Pasenadi?'

'We dare not refuse the Kosalas,' Bhalatiya, one of the *amalas*, sounded apprehensive.

'We need to bear in mind that if we refuse Pasenadi, their army being stronger than ours may pound us to defeat,' articulated Harita, the oldest *amala* of them all. 'Nayak Mahanama, we need to come to a coherent solution.'

'I have a plan if only you all agree to it,' said Mahanama.

'And what plan is this, Mahanama?'

'You all know of Vasabhakhatiya, my daughter from my *dasi* Nagamunda. She is very pretty; you all have seen her. She is graceful too and fit to be the Maharani of Kosala. We can easily pose her as a Sakya princess and send her to Savathi to marry Maharaj Pasenadi.' Mahanama paused a little and then resumed, 'Having no other option, I feel that we should all agree to this.'

All the officers talked among themselves. Then old Harita put in a word of caution, 'Mahanama, have you thought of the consequence of such a deceit? What if Pasenadi gets to know about her real identity? Would it not be disastrous for Kapilavatthu?'

'My dear old Harita, calamity nonetheless hovers on us if we refuse to send Pasenadi a Sakya rajkumari. I would never, by any chance, offer one my own daughters' hands in marriage with the low-born Pasenadi. So what other options are we left with?'

'True,' everyone echoed in unison.

'Do you then agree to my decision of sending my daughter from my slave to Savathi for the wedding?' Silence once again descended among the councillors, while a few conversed grimly with one another.

'Well, it seems that we do not have other alternatives.'

'Is it decided then?' asked Mahanama to his councillors.

'Yes,' everyone voiced in agreement.

'Now I would want all the *amalas* to see Vasabhakhatiya, whom we have agreed to send to marry Pasenadi and become the Queen of Kosala,' remarked Mahanama. He called for Nagamunda who, along with her daughter Vasabhakhatiya, was standing in complete silence and teary eyes along the inner doorway of the *santhagara*. Every word that was spoken by her master and his *amalas* inside the *parishad kuti* of the *santhagara* reached her ears, and she wordlessly endured the humiliation. Trembling with fear, Nagamunda looked at her young and artless daughter. If caught, Vasabhakhatiya would be hanged for a crime that her father and his councillors were forcing her to commit.

Nagamunda's master Mahanama had instructed her to embellish Vasabhakhatiya so charmingly that the aged *amartyas* would gawk at her beauty flabbergasted, and approve Mahanama's arrangement. When Nagamunda courted her daughter into the *parishad kuti*, everyone indeed looked at her in stunned silence. Mahanama knew at that very moment that he had succeeded in his plan.

'Isn't she the right one?' asked Mahanama.

'Yes, she is!' the councillors rejoined in agreement.

'Alright then, we move according to my plan. But everyone should remember that the decision of this arrangement should not escape the walls of our *santhagara*, or else we are doomed. With such a plan, we guard our pride and dignity of being a Sakya,' warned Mahanama. Everyone inside the chamber consented. 'That would be all. Nagamunda, take her away now,' directed Mahanama.

As the two women walked away, they overheard an *amala* observe, 'She indeed is beautiful, suitable to be the Maharani of Kosala. Maharaj Pasenadi, even in his wildest dreams, would never know that she is a *dasi-putri*. Ha ha ha....'

***

That night, Vasabhakhatiya saw her mother standing in the waning light of the *ekadasi* moon that rose in the night of the western sky, faintly illuminating the lampless courtyard. Nagamunda was gazing at the woods in the faraway foot of the Himalayas.

'Mai,' Vasabhakhatiya called. Nagamunda pulled her daughter to her bosom. Running her fingers through her daughter's hair, she spoke softly, 'There in the distant forest near the mountain was the village where I once lived. I do not know whether my parents are still alive. My brothers, my sisters, and my friends ... wonder where they are now. I want to go there, my girl ... to see my mother, my father ... ' Vasabhakhatiya felt warm teardrops on her cheeks; she found her mother weeping.

'How did you come here, Mother?' Vasabhakhatiya asked.

'When he was young, your father had attacked our village along with other Sakyas. The men abducted the womenfolk and brought them here. Your father took me and put me in a dilapidated house where a few other *dasi*s were already kept. I have never been home since. Later, when you were born, he built this house for me.' Nagamunda wiped her eyes and then, looking at Vasabhakhatiya, said sympathetically, 'Vasu, my child, very soon you too would leave me. Neither have I given you a decent life, nor would I be giving you a respectable marriage. Your father is marrying you off to the King of Kosala, masquerading you as the Rajkumari of Kapilavatthu to become his Maharani. They are using you deliberately to offend Pasenadi. I hope you can understand how much this hurts me, for I cannot do anything to stop it. I am so worried, my girl. In case the truth is exposed, what happens then? I cannot object to this marriage. I am not free to do so ... I am just a slave woman.' She continued to weep.

Gripped with terror at the idea of getting caught in Savathi for faking to be the princess of Kapilavatthu, Vasabhakhatiya felt no delight or excitement at the idea of becoming the queen of Kosala after her marriage to Maharaja Pasenadi.

'Mother, I am frightened,' she said, trembling. The moonlight in the verandah unexpectedly dimmed. A dark cloud had shrouded the moon.

The form of a woman, bhikkhus, overpowers the mind of a man. The form of a man, bhikkhus, overpowers the mind of a woman.

—**Rūpādi Vagga**

News was conveyed to Maharaja Pasenadi that Mahanama, the nayaka of Kapilavatthu, has consented to give Rajkumari Vasabhakhatiya in marriage to the maharaja of Kosala. In the process, the truth was obviously concealed that she was not a rajkumari but his daughter from his *dasi*. Pasenadi, naive of this deception, was jubilant to marry a princess of the Sakya dynasty and thereby establish a relationship with his most revered Sakyamuni, the Buddha.

Kosala was all decked out to receive its second queen from the Sakyas, as its citizens too were delighted to strike a kinship with the Buddha's own people, the Sakyas. Various festivities were held in the city and even within the palace. Though Mallika was unable to get rid of her guilt for not being able to give birth to the prince of Kosala, she too was strangely delighted for the wedding of her husband to another woman, whom she trusted would surely deliver the future prince.

Mallika received Vasabhakhatiya warmly. Vasabhakhatiya was led to the royal guest house where she was to reside till her wedding with Maharaja Pasenadi on an auspicious date set by the royal astrologers.

The marriage was finally solemnized with much pomp and splendour on the decided propitious date. The whole of Savathi was celebrating. Bimbisara, the king of Magadha, his queen Kosala Devi, and other kings and rajas of different kingdoms and *ganarajyas* were among the various prominent guests in the royal wedding. Mahanama, the father of Vasabhakhatiya, along with a few other eminent Sakyas, were special guests for the occasion. The Buddha and his *sangha*, however, were untraceable and hence could not be invited. It disappointed Maharaja Pasenadi and Maharani Mallika, as the marriage had to be initiated without his blessings.

Resting in their allotted rooms in Savathi, Mahanama and his *amalas* were anxious in fear of the expose of the deceit. Fortunately, for them, it did not. After the marriage, Mallika gladly escorted the new queen Rani Vasabhakhatiya to the king's bedroom. Even if she did nurture a trace of envy against Vasabhakhatiya, Mallika's features did not betray it.

A honeymoon boat ride for a few days on the Achiravati River beginning the following day was arranged for the newly wedded royal couple. The boat that was rowed leisurely on the river by four oarsmen was garnished discerningly with sweet-smelling flowers that attracted several honeybees and butterflies. The king's guards and attendants trailed the royal boat in a separate vessel, while the royal couple spent their days and nights in solitude in each other's arms, gazing lazily at the gliding birds on the river and even witnessing the magnificent view of the setting sun in the western horizon.

In no time, Vasabhakhatiya formed a niche in Pasenadi's heart. She conceived the very first year. The *rajjyotishi* was called for to decipher the gender of the maharaja's next issue from the new rani. Studying the horoscopes, the *rajjyotishi* predicted that the newborn would be a son.

'Are you sure of this?' asked Maharaja Pasenadi.

'Maharaj, have any of my predictions been erroneous till now?'

The king instructed the elderly women of the palace to take special care of the pregnant queen. Strong directives were issued, warning that negligence of the queen's upkeep would not be tolerated as she bore the future king of Kosala.

When the time came, she delivered a beautiful male heir.

Maharaja Pasenadi entered the *aturghar* where the queen and her newborn were resting. They would have to stay there for the next twenty-one days. Beside Vasabhakhatiya's bed sat Maharani Mallika and the aunts of the maharaja. Male members other than the king were barred from entering the room. Pasenadi found the newborn sleeping next to his mother.

'Are you happy?' Vasabhakhatiya asked the king delightfully.

'More than anything, My Queen!' replied Pasenadi smilingly. The father bent to examine his son.

'He is like you,' the king remarked, kissing his son's forehead.

'He is like you,' said Mallika, who was standing beside Vasabhakhatiya's bed, gazing at the newborn and his father.

'I am so proud and happy to be the father of the future king of Kosala,' announced Pasenadi.

***

It was time for celebration once again in Savathi. The capital was decorated with flowers and lit with lamps. Month-long singing and dancing were organized in almost all the squares of the city. Animals and children performed acrobatics, while the *madaris*, magicians, and singers performed in the streets. Feasts were organized in the palace for which countless animals were slaughtered. Gifts were offered to Brahmins and other ascetics. News of the prince's birth was transmitted and precious gifts sent to the kings of the various *mahajanapadas* and to the nayakas of the different *ganarajyas*. The news also reached Kapilavatthu.

On a late afternoon, Mahanama softly traipsed his way to Nagamunda's. The door was opened by her maidservant, who, seeing the raja of Kapilavatthu at the door, bowed to him and moved aside to let him enter. Mahanama settled on his usual *chowki* near the window in the front room.

'You have come after so many days,' Nagamunda quipped, as she emerged from the inner room to touch her master's feet.

'I have some good news for you, Naga,' Mahanama said placidly.

'What is it, Master?' asked Nagamunda. The Sakya chief displayed a broad grin, which he hadn't done in many years.

'Naga, my dear, you are now a grandmother. Our Vasu has given birth to a bonny boy, the future king of Kosala.'

Nagamunda remained quiet for a while. Then she raised her clasped hands to her forehead to thank Sin Bonga and Goddess Abhaya. Her visage lit with joy, a joy she had never perceived before. She had not anticipated such a news.

'Please wait, I shall get some sweets for you.' Nagamunda sent her maid to get some sweets. In a while, the female attendant appeared with some jaggery on a stone platter. Mahanama put a small slice of it into his mouth and a large piece into Nagamunda's.

'I presume that the fear of Vasu being caught is stalled for a little while,' said Mahanama. Hearing this, Nagamunda's ecstasy disappeared as the reality suddenly hit her. Her eyes gazed through the western window towards Savathi.

'Is Vasu still living in fear or has her son brought happiness in her life?' Nagamunda speculated as she shut her eyes and tears rolled down her cheeks.

Rising from his *chowki*, Mahanama patted the shoulder of Nagamunda and then slowly walked out of the house.

***

Colourful stones, beads, and crystals in ancient times were called *vidudabha* in the early societies. Extremely expensive, these were held in the highest esteem, perhaps because the ancients believed that the stones possessed mystical powers. The newborn prince, too, was a rare and an expensive crystal for the dynasty and for Kosala; hence, he was named Vidudabha by the king's old aunt Pano.

He should not kill a living being, nor cause it to be killed, nor should he incite another to kill.

—**Sutta Nipata**

Tathagata and his *sangha* trekked slowly from Veshali towards the Gijjhakuta Hill in Rajagaha. The highway, after the rains, had become too rugged to walk on. The *bhikkhus*, therefore, chose a narrow trail through an open field to reach Rajagaha. Arriving at a small village, they spotted a large verdant banyan. Moggallana suggested that they rest there for the day. A little farther, they observed a large house that perhaps belonged to a wealthy man. Beside the banyan was a beautiful mango tree where a large number of buffaloes were tethered under its cool shade. On enquiring, they learnt that the beasts were about to be sacrificed in a yagna by the rich man of that house.

The *bhikkhus* set off for their *pindapata* in the village. When news of the arrival of the Buddha spread, the villagers thronged to see him. In this swarm of people was also an overweight, middle-aged man, who incidentally was the owner of the big house that the Buddha and his *sangha* had seen earlier in front of the banyan.

'O Master, it is an honour for us that you happen to be here in our village, and that too near my house,' the rich man said, folding his palms together in supplication. Then he fell on the Buddha's feet and kissed them. The villagers followed suit. Tathagata raised his right palm to bestow his blessings.

'Master, I shall be conducting a yagna in a few days' time. Brahmin priests shall soon be arriving here from Haridwar, Ujjain, and Kashi. O, Venerated One, I request you and your *sangha* to stay and preside over the ceremony,' the rich man pleaded.

'Your yagna will be performed in the future. The future is unknown and uncertain. So my stay depends on the morrow,' said the Buddha. Thereafter, turning towards the tethered animals, he questioned the rich man, 'What are those animals meant for?'

'Master, they will be sacrificed in the yagna.'

'Why do you wish to have them sacrificed, Sir?'

'The sacrifices of these buffaloes in the yagna will appease the evil planets and even purge their bad effects, for such bad energies obstruct the good influences that reach my family,' replied the man.

'Sir, the planets are in the space beyond the earth. How can they bring good or bad luck? How can the sacrifice of buffaloes stop or shower fortune from space? Obstacles and time, be they good or bad, are a constituent of life; they are bound to happen as results of the various *kamma*s we do,' remonstrated the Buddha. The rich man did not respond.

'Impermanence is the chief trait of life. The world is synonymous with suffering, which is a part of every life, and each *dukkha* stems from one's attachment to greed and desire. This thirst of greed and desire grow from being unsatisfied with ourselves and also from the ignorance of the self. We shall keep on taking birth in this earth to suffer till we do not put an end to the effects of the various *kamma*s we perform.

'The termination of suffering or *dukkha* can be done if we follow eight proper *magga*s or paths of right view, right conduct, right living, right speech, right effort, right consciousness, right meditation, and right intention. Clinging to material things that we think give us happiness actually results in more *dukkha* and suffering. Therefore, non-attachment towards material desires, which is also a right effort, will definitely help you end your sufferings.' Sitting in the *vitarka mudra* with the tips of his thumb and index finger touching each other in a circle, The Venerated One spoke both to the rich man and the people who had gathered to listen to him. Womenfolk had already begun pouring in, bringing with them a range of food for the Buddha and his *sangha*. The rich man was listening intently with folded hands.

Tathagata continued, 'Always speak the truth and never resort to lying. Avoid gossip, never steal, and do not get involved in wrongful sexual activities. Shed anger and envy. Always think of others' pain, be it humans or animals, and never cause them harm. Do not sacrifice innocent animals, as their slaughter can never help in reducing or obliterating your sufferings or *dukkha*. Your *dukkha* comes from your bad *kamma*. Whenever you get time, do not waste it by whiling away your hours, but meditate to find the truth inside you. Remember that happiness comes not from external sources but from within. I know it is difficult as it will take time for you to properly understand these. But when you do and apply them in your life, they would help in the cessation of your *dukkha*.

'Finally Brothers, I pray that no one deceives or despises the other or wishes harm to another out of anger or hatred. May all be detached from the desires of the senses. Remember, the world to which we are so intensely attached is an abode of misery where we keep returning by taking births. If attachment is the root of all sufferings, then non-attachment saves us from it as it liberates all from the cycle of rebirth. May you all radiate your kindness to the entire existence—humans, animals, birds, trees, rivers, hills, everything. May all living beings be compassionate and happy.'

The villagers were listening to Gautama's sermons with

profound attentiveness. His discourse made a deep impression on the fat wealthy man, who sat still for a long time, even after the sermon had ended. Then, rising slowly, he walked towards the Buddha and fell on his feet, drenching them with his tears. 'My Lord, your words have sunk deep into me ... never shall I indulge in wrongful means to end my problems. Forgive me, O Master, as I have wronged. I shall tell my sons to set these animals free right now,' the rich man grieved, holding his palms together before the Buddha.

It soon became dark. Buddha instructed his *sangha* to sit for their dhyana.

Early the following morning, they started for the Gijjhakuta Hill in Rajagaha and reached there by late afternoon. Arriving at the city, Kassapa heard the news of the birth of Vidudabha and immediately conveyed it to Gautama.

The mind is unstable and flighty. It wanders wherever it desires. A well-guarded mind brings happiness.

—**Dhammapada**

After court, the king retreated to his inner quarters. He longed to cuddle his son. As Pasenadi walked towards his room, Vidudabha's giggles resounded in the corridor, bringing joy to his heart. Although many years had passed since Vidudabha's birth, Pasenadi still felt that he was born only the other day. Entering his room, Pasenadi found his son playing with both the queens, Vasabhakhatiya and Mallika. Vajira, his daughter, was also playing with her half-brother.

'Babu, babu, please scold didi. She is pinching me,' seeing his father enter, Vidudabha complained to him while jumping onto his lap. Pasenadi pulled his son close and gave him a long kiss.

'Didi pinched you, did she? It is indeed bad, Yuvraj. I shall surely punish her,' Pasenadi wiggled his nose on his son's belly as the little prince burst into peals of laughter.

***

Vidudabha was growing up fast into a handsome boy, but all the pampering spoiled him so that he became rude and arrogant. This worried his mother Vasabhakhatiya.

'Such pompousness is good for a king. With the turn of events and the state of affairs in the nearby kingdoms and *ganarajyas*, Kosala will need a strong and resolute king in the future to handle difficult situations,' Pasenadi told Vasabhakhatiya, laughing her apprehensions away.

Down the years, the young rajkumar, under the supervision of Senapati Digha Karayana, was gradually maturing into a fine horse rider and a great fencer.

***

Late afternoon.

Pasenadi was in his assembly when Vadana, the informant, arrived fretfully and approached Sudatta, the prime minister. He murmured something into Sudatta's ears, whose face soon turned tense.

'What is it?' enquired the king.

'Maharaj,' the prime minister replied. 'Vadana brings very disquieting news.'

'Speak,' ordered the king.

'Your Highness, Maharaj Bimbisara, your brother-in-law, has been imprisoned by his son Ajatsattu, who has declared himself the king of Magadha.'

'This is terrible news! How is my sister?' asked Pasenadi.

'Maharaj, although we do not have much news of her, some reports suggest that she is alright,' responded the minister.

'That is a relief,' said Pasenadi with a deep sigh. Then he continued, 'Ajat was a good lad. He was to inherit his father's throne. So what was the need to commit such an evil act?'

'We have news that this conspiracy of Ajatsattu to imprison his father was hatched at the behest of Devadatta, the cousin of Tathagata. A few days ago, Devadatta had even attacked Tathagata. Lucky for all of us that the *vaidya* Jivaka attended to him and cured his wounds,' reported the informant. Pasenadi's face now displayed restrained anger.

'How is the Master now?'

'Maharaj, he has recovered.'

After a moment of silence, Maharaja Pasenadi turned towards his minister and instructed, 'Minister, order our Senapati to be vigilant at the border lest Ajatsattu, coerced by Devadatta, may attempt some misadventure.'

'Yes, Maharaj.'

'Messenger, I want more news of Kosala Devi by tomorrow morning. Get busy with your people right now.'

'Yes, Your Majesty,' replied the informant and rushed out of the room.

The next morning did bring good news. Kosala Devi, along with the rest of the queens of Bimbisara, was safe.

According to the king's command, Digha Karayana had his army positioned on standby at the border between Kosala and Magadha, in case an attack was attempted by the Magadha army on Kosala. Meanwhile, the chief minister of Kosala, along with the council of ministers and advisers, sat in consultation with Maharani Mallika and Maharaja Pasenadi to discuss on how to protect Kosala Devi, the daughter of Kosala, from any threats by her son Ajatsattu. A wait and watch policy was adopted and an understanding was reached that the Kosala intelligence inside the palace of Rajagaha was required to be reinforced and that Kosala Devi's news was to reach Savathi every day. In case she was subjected to any form of maltreatment, an attack on Magadha would become imminent.

However, things at Magadha gradually limped back to normalcy in a few days. Kosala Devi remained unharmed at Rajagaha.

There is no fear for one whose mind is not filled with desires.

—Dhammapada

News of a sudden rebellion popping up its head in Tandwa, which lay to the south of Kosala close to the frontier of the *mahajanapada* of Vatsya, reached Savathi. The region was always a hotbed of such uprisings.

'What is the unrest about, Minister?' asked Pasenadi anxiously.

'Maharaj,' the minister replied, 'it is their customary demand to form their own *ganarajya* by disassociating themselves from Kosala.'

'Did they not revolt twice during the reign of my father?'

'Yes Sire, but this time we have been informed that they have the patronage of the Vatsyas. The revolt is indeed stronger this time. They have gutted many shops and homes. They have even decided not to pay levies. Their demand is to attain complete independence from us.'

Pasenadi called upon an emergency meeting that included the minister, senapati, advisors, and officers, the agenda being the quashing of the rebellion.

'Your Honour, if you permit me I could make a suggestion,' said Mahidal, one of the superior officers.

'Speak up, Officer.'

'Maharaj, your friend Bandhula, the former nayak of Kusinara whom you have appointed as the Minister of the Food Department, was once an accomplished warrior of Kusinara. Can we not use his service in settling the uprising?' Mahidal made a very vital proposal.

'Yes, that indeed is a very wise suggestion, officer,' Pasenadi resounded loudly, thumping on his throne. He continued, 'Bandhula has performed many difficult tasks with considerable success. He does seem to be a right choice to quell the rebellion.'

The ministers, advisors, and the other officials seconded the idea, but oddly Senapati Digha remained silent.

'Well, Senapati, are you not happy with the decision of sending Bandhula to Tandwa?'

'Actually Maharaj, I am not,' Digha was firm in his reply.

'Senapati, I presume that Bandhula is the right man for this challenging task. He has handled many such arduous assignments in Kusinara with great success.'

'As you suggest, Maharaj,' Digha responded softly, for he knew very well that opposing the king's decision now was a pointless attempt.

Bandhula, who once was the nayaka of the Malla *ganarajya*, was also the schoolmate of Pasenadi at Takshashila. Being a follower of the Buddha's *dhamma*, he was a man of truth and integrity, and under him Kusinara had flourished immensely. Sadly, a conspiracy that brewed against his life forced him to flee the country with his family and seek asylum at Savathi, where Pasenadi received him jubilantly with open arms. Learning of Bandhula's moral fibre, Mallika recommended that he be appointed the Minister of Food and Supplies, as they were unable to put a check on the corrupt practices of the officials in the department.

'Bandhula, my friend, the corrupt officials are everywhere, particularly in the food supply department. Food from our *bhandar* is not reaching the indigent and the underprivileged. Constant theft of food from the *bhandar* is rampant, and it seems difficult to put a curb on this. Furthermore, a proper distribution of food is also not being carried out. As advised by Maharani Mallika, I wish to appoint you as the Minister of Food and Supplies so that you can put an end to the dishonest practices prevailing there,' the king had said.

'Maharaj, I'd be happy in accepting the job,' replied Bandhula.

'My officers will explain to you the details of the work, but Bandhula, my friend, see that corruption is comprehensively wiped out and my people are served well.'

'I shall indeed try my best, O King, to return the favour you have done to my family and myself,' Bandhula answered, accepting the new responsibility in Savathi. Changes became clearly visible in the department within a few days, as Bandhula executed his responsibility with utmost finesse and severity. All the grievances amongst the needy gradually began to cease, as distribution was suitably redressed with food reaching the impoverished the most. He marked the officers responsible for pilfering food and absolved them from their duties, which made him an obvious target of rage, envy, and malice.

The dishonest and the crooked having lost their fraudulent earnings joined hands to seek vengeance against Bandhula. Eventually, their opportunity came during the uprising in Tandwa. The idea among the retrenched officials was that, if in some way, they could convince Pasenadi to send Bandhula away from Savathi and then somehow impede his return, the recommencing of their rapacious malpractices in the food department would not be much of a hitch.

***

Maharaja Pasenadi summoned Bandhula, who appeared at his friend and king Pasenadi's beckoning.

'Bandhula, my friend, a problem has cropped up in Kosala. I, in person, being conscious of your accomplishments in Kusinara, seek your assistance in dealing with it,' said Pasenadi.

'What is it, Maharaj?' asked Bandhula very courteously. Pasenadi told him about the uprising. 'We, in Kosala, know what a great warrior you are; we are aware of your extraordinary diplomatic techniques in checking a rebellion. Therefore, Bandhula, my mate, we seek your service in suppressing a mutiny that has risen in Tandwa,' Pasenadi placed the proposal before Bandhula very candidly.

'You are free to use any means to repeal the sedition, diplomacy or violence whatever. I want results. A large troop of soldiers will accompany you to Tandwa, but I cannot send Senapati Digha with you as he is monitoring the Magadha border where a situation of turmoil lingers after Bimbisara's imprisonment.'

Bandhula could very well perceive that Pasenadi had fallen prey to a conspiracy hatched by the corrupt officials to get rid of him, so that they could resume their fraudulent practices in his absence. Burdened under the gratitude of his friend, Bandhula put forth no resistance and silently accepted the king's proposal. He left for Tandwa early next morning with a large contingent of soldiers.

Not to be associated with the foolish ones, to live in the company of wise people and honouring those who are worth honouring—this is the greatest happiness.

—Mangala Sutta

The officials, wicked and unethical to their core, had succeeded in their clandestine design to remove the honest Bandhula not only from the Department of Food Supplies but also from Savathi. Now their next move was to have him secretly exterminated, lest he returned and persisted to be a plaguing impediment in their path of siphoning money into their own *thaila*s.

After his departure, the sycophant officials fed Pasenadi lies about how Bandhula was stealing food and illicitly selling it at low rates to the Mallas in Kusinara. The conspirators presented false evidences to the king in support of their allegations, and Pasenadi, without even verifying the verity of these accusations against Bandhula, decidedly believed in his officers.

'This is despicable! I cannot believe that Bandhula, my childhood friend, whom I entrusted with such a big responsibility can do this to Kosala. I am so distressed! He should be punished by any means,' thundered an enraged Pasenadi.

'He should not return, Your Highness.'

'Let him quell the rebellion first, then he shall pay for his sins,' retorted Pasenadi.

As anticipated, Bandhula suppressed the rebellion without any bloodshed. The populace of Tandwa pinned their faith on him and ended their uprising after being assured that their problems shall be heard by Kosala *naresh*.

A tent was pitched for Bandhula in the outskirts of Tandwa to spend his night. Since it was summer, his soldiers slept in the open. Bandhula, being a disciple of the Buddha, performed dhyana each night before sleeping. That night, exhausted due to the long and tiring day, Bandhula fell asleep immediately after his supper and meditation.

Not a leaf moved in the warm summer night, while the waning *veshak* moon glowed dimly in the north-westerly sky. A flimsy human shadow moved slowly amidst the snores and grunts of the soldiers, and tiptoed softly into the tent of Bandhula. Once inside, the man crept to Bandhula's bed. With intense force, he covered Bandhula's mouth with his left hand; then he fished out a dagger with his right hand and slashed Bandhula's throat. He let out a restrained groan; then, quivering a little, Bandhula fell silent, forever. Blood gushed out of his throat as his lifeless body lay on the bed.

The shadow sneaked out silently from the tent as he had entered.

Around the same time, in the stillness of the night, four men broke into Bandhula's home in Savathi. One gagged Bandhula's wife, lest she screamed, while the rest slaughtered all her children in front of her eyes. Then, without a sound, the men sneaked out of the house. The following morning, Pasenadi and his officials were content with jobs so neatly done.

***

Digha Karayana, the senapati of Kosala, silently observed the wrongs Pasenadi committed against Bandhula and his family. By submitting to the conspiracy of the corrupt officials, the king had an innocent man and his children massacred as a punishment for a crime he had never committed. Bandhula happened to be Digha's maternal uncle. After the sudden demise of his parents, Digha was raised by Bandhula as his own son. Digha literally worshipped the ground his uncle walked on. The carnage of Bandhula and his children committed at the order of Pasenadi resulted in supreme revulsion in the heart of Digha against the king. Somehow containing his anger, he waited patiently for the right time and opportunity to avenge their deaths, which incidentally was to come in a few years' time.

If a man commits evil let him not repeat it again and again; let him not delight in it, for the accumulation of sin brings suffering.

—Dhammapada

The realization that he had committed a grave blunder by coming under the influence of the corrupt officials and having the honest Bandhula and his children exterminated eventually came to Pasenadi. Stung by profound remorse, Maharaja Pasenadi was having sleepless and restless nights.

'What did I do, Mallika? Why did I not authenticate the reality of the entire episode from the very mouth of my dear friend Bandhula? Never did he once resist my command to go to Tandwa; instead, as a true friend, he consented immediately to travel there and crushed the mutiny successfully. I disbelieved him and had him killed by trusting my evil officers. Maharani, what have I done?' Breaking down, Pasenadi admitted his guilt to Mallika.

'Remember the words of Tathagata: "Why should we do unfair deeds to which we later regret and bring tears upon ourselves?" How true the Master is about everything, O Maharaj,' replied Mallika.

'True, Maharani, even the Buddha isn't here to guide me. What should I do now to make amends for my offences that may bring solace to my restless heart?'

'Your friend Bandhula was a true follower of The Enlightened One, and he remained honest to his duty as long as he served you. Maharaj, firstly punish the corrupt officials who instigated you to have him killed. Then go to Bandhula's wife and beg her forgiveness for your evil act. If she ever pardons you, Maharaj, I reckon your restiveness may subside that day.'

***

As suggested by Maharani Mallika, Maharaja Pasenadi immediately ordered the arrest of Mahidal and other corrupt officials who had persuaded the king to commit this felony. They were subsequently hanged by the order of the king.

Mustering up moral courage, one morning Pasenadi personally called on Mallika, the wife of the deceased Bandhula, whose children were slaughtered in front of her eyes. Opening the door, Mallika found the king standing at the entrance.

'My *johar* to you,' Pasenadi bowed to Mallika guiltily.

'My *johar*, Maharaj. What is it that I can do for you?' asked Mallika. Pasenadi found her dressed in an orange robe; it seemed that she had become a *bhikkhuni* of the Buddha's *sangha*.

'I am your offender of the ghastly crimes against your husband and children. My wrongs, I know, can never be forgiven; yet I am here, O *bhikkhuni*, to receive any punishment that you may bestow on me,' Pasenadi stood in front of Mallika, looking down in shame.

'I have no resentment against you, Maharaj. I have already forgiven you. I have dedicated my life to the *sangha* of the Buddha, and I bid farewell to all my attachments. I was about to leave my house forever when you knocked. Please permit me now to depart in the search of truth,' Mallika said submissively with folded hands.

Tears of penitence filled Pasenadi's eyes as he moved aside to give way to the *bhikkhuni*. She walked out of her home in search of bliss.

The world is afflicted by death and decay. But the wise do not grieve, having realized the nature of the world.

—Sutta Nipata

Whenever in Rajagaha, whether alone or with his favourite disciple and cousin Ananda or his other disciples, Tathagata would reside in a cave in the Gijjhakuta Hill. Maharaja Bimbisara had constructed a stone house close to the base of the hill in order to get a glimpse of the Buddha scaling the hill in the distance. When Bimbisara found that Tathagata's age was making it difficult for him to climb, he built stairs from the foot of the hill to the cave to make his mount easy. It was eventually in this dwelling that Ajatsattu confined his father Bimbisara. Bimbisara's anguish in being held captive by his son in that stone house was somewhat lessened by the sight of his beloved Buddha walking up the hill.

One afternoon in Savathi, Vadana, the royal secret informer, arrived at the assembly in haste. 'What news do you bring, messenger?' asked the king.

'I have some bad news, Maharaj,' replied Vadana.

'Speak up fast.'

'Maharaj, the imprisoned former king of Magadha and Kosala's brother-in-law, the great Bimbisara, has shed his earthly attire and departed for his heavenly abode.'

It was as if lightning had abruptly dropped on the maharaja and his assembly.

After a moment of silence, the maharaja said, 'I had been expecting this. Now tell me, how is my sister Devi?'

'We have reports that she is taken ill.'

'No!' exclaimed the king. This time, the silence in the assembly was longer. The king then looked at his minister.

'Shall we attack Magadha, My Lord?' asked Sudatta.

'Hmm ... not now, Minister,' Pasenadi replied grimly. 'We need to be vigilant for a while. What is occurring there now would be their internal matter. It shall not be proper for us to meddle in it. But, in case anything untoward happens to Devi, we should not wait to declare war on Magadha.' Pasenadi then turned towards Vadana and directed him, 'Informer, instruct your men to keep me reported on Kosala Devi's condition twice every day.'

By the next afternoon, news reached Savathi that Kosala Devi, unable to bear the death of her husband, has taken to bed. *Vaidyas* were attending to her, but her health did not show signs of improvement. Later in the evening, Pasenadi sat pensively in his room with his two queens. Vajira was running her fingers in her father's long hair, while Pasenadi rested, reclining in his seat, his eyes closed. Vidudabha walked into the room after completing his evening studies under a Brahmin tutor. Finding his father in deep contemplation and everyone else in grim silence, he asked his mother, 'Why is everyone so silent, Mai?' No one responded; Vasabhakhatiya signalled her son to remain quiet.

'Viru, my brother, Aunt Devi, the Maharani of Magadha, has taken ill,' Vajira told her brother while stroking her father's head. Vidudabha, who was in his early teens by now, understood the gravity of the matter and said no more.

***

The next morning, bad news arrived. Kosala Devi was dead.

Though one were to conquer a million men in battle, that man who conquers himself is the greater victor.

—Dhammapada

It was night-time.

Two lamps glowed inside the *sabhakuti*, casting a pale yellow tinge of light all over the room. Yet, darkness prevailed in the corners, creating an aura of mystery. Maharaja Pasenadi, Senapati Digha, and Chief Minister Sudatta sat closely to chalk out a plan for their future course of action. An atmosphere of indignation was apparent. Pasenadi held his nephew Ajatsattu responsible for his sister Kosala Devi's death; now he sought revenge. All the advisors agreed that there was no other option than to attack Magadha in retaliation to Devi's fatality.

***

Through the window of a room in the third floor of the palace, Yuvraj Vidudabha gazed at a large contingent of the Kosala army that had assembled in the wide open field adjacent to the encircling moat of the palace. The army was drawn up in ranks. The infantry stood in rows, armed with bows and arrows, spears, talwars, and *dhals*. The troop also comprised of an assortment of artillery such as the *vasi pharasukan*, *pasana mugara*, *ayo mugara*, and *khuradharan chakkavishan* (war weapons used in ancient India). The large cavalry on horseback and chariots stood behind the infantry, donning *talwars*, bows and arrows, and other weapons.

An army about to go to a battle was a sight that provided immense pleasure to young Vidudabha. The adolescent prince fostered a deep longing to witness a war and bloodshed someday. A clamour rapidly rose among the soldiers. The reason behind it was not clear. Vidudabha soon found the reason for the commotion as he looked the other way. Pasenadi, the king of Kosala, had arrived to ascend his chariot. Alongside the king was Digha Karayana, the senapati.

'Yuvraj, are you there?' A female aide entered the room searching for Vidudabha and found him looking out of the window. Rani Vasabhakhatiya too came inside. 'What are you watching, dear?' she asked.

'I am looking at Baba and his army preparing go to war against Magadha,' replied Vidudabha. At that moment, Vajira too walked into the room to find both Vidudabha and his mother staring out of the window. 'What are you both looking at, Choti Mai?' asked Rajkumari Vajira.

'The king heads for war against your cousin Ajatsattu, Vajira,' answered Vasabhakhatiya.

'How I detest wars and killings!' Vajira exclaimed, looking at the large band of soldiers.

'But I love wars. Someday, I too shall fight when I become the king of Kosala,' young Vidudabha replied absent-mindedly. Vajira stared at her younger brother to find self-assurance and poise reflecting in his youthful eyes.

***

The battle between Magadha and Kosala did not last long. It wrapped up in a few days. Despite having a larger army and war weapons like *mahshila kantaka* and *rathamusala*, Ajatsattu lacked the insight of his father, the experienced Bimbisara, due to which Magadha suffered an overwhelming defeat in the hands of the skilled Pasenadi. Ajatsattu was taken into custody and brought to Savathi.

Vidudabha woke up with a start as his half-sister Vajira nudged him, 'Wake up, Viru, wake up.'

'What is it, Didi?' Vidudabha quickly sat up in his bed, rubbing his eyes.

'Baba has returned victorious. He has brought our cousin Ajatsattu as his prisoner. Come, let's go and see him.'

Getting to see a prisoner is a matter of curiosity for all, more so for youngsters.

'Where is he, Didi?' asked Vidudabha.

'Perhaps in the king's court. Come, let's go fast.'

Running across the corridors, they finally arrived at the large assembly where Maharaja Pasenadi sat with poise and composure with both his queens by his side. Standing beside the thick columns, the first thing they spotted was their cousin Ajatsattu, the king of Magadha who, although was not handcuffed like an ordinary prisoner, sat sulking on a seat a little further from their father's throne. Food was served to him on a stone dish that contained some leftovers and a clay tumbler with water was kept beside it.

The courtier suddenly stood up, clutching a rolled-up *bhojpatra*. He unfurled it and began reading out loud and clear so that he was audible in the entire hall. They were the allegations directed at the king of Magadha.

'Ajatsattu, Maharaj of Magadha, you are now a prisoner in the court of the mighty King Pasenadi of Kosala. You being the king's nephew, our great Maharaj Pasenadi has displayed his magnanimity by not having you chained and arrested like a common prisoner. Our noble Maharaj has also exhibited his generosity by allowing you to sit close to him as his royal guest, even though you are Kosala's prisoner defeated in a battle against our king.'

Although young, Vidudabha was sensible enough to understand every word being spoken by the courtier. The young prince fixed his gaze at his cousin Ajatsattu, who was wiping his sweaty face in the hot and humid weather.

'Ajatsattu,' the announcer continued. 'The following charges have been levelled against you. You are a parricide. You imprisoned your father, the great Bimbisara, and let him die in prison. You forgot that Maharaj Bimbisara is also the brother-in-law of Maharaj Pasenadi.

'Owing to your evil deed, your mother, the great Maharani Kosala Devi, the sister of our magnificent Maharaj Pasenadi, died in distress. To punish you for your malevolent actions, Kosala declared war against you in which your army has been severely trounced and you have been brought here to Savathi as a prisoner. Magadha has, therefore, been brought under the command of our eminent Maharaj Pasenadi of the mighty Kosala. Ajatsattu, you shall be kept inside a room as a guest despite being a prisoner, till it is decided what is to be done with you.'

At that instant, a sentry came running inside the court and declared, 'The Sakymuni, along with his *sangha*, is arriving at the king's court.'

A mind unruffled by the vagaries of fortune, from sorrow freed, from defilements cleansed, from fear liberated—this is the greatest blessing.

—Mangala Sutta

Maharaja Pasenadi and both his queens hurried towards the palace entrance to welcome Tathagata. Vajira and her brother Vidudabha, too, rushed out with their parents. The officials of the Kosala court stood outside to receive the Buddha. All eyes were fixed on the old, saffron-robed *bhikkhu* in the distance, with a begging bowl in one hand and a stick in the other, slowly advancing towards the palace. His demeanour revealed tranquillity and calmness, suggesting that he indeed was the Blessed One. The princess, the queens, and the king touched the feet of the Buddha reverently. Prince Vidudabha, too, fell at his feet to kiss them, even though he did not admire the Buddha much.

'Maharaj, I hope everything is fine here,' Tathagata asked the king smilingly, holding his hands.

'By your grace, O Enlightened One, we all are fine here.'

'I have been told that you fought a war with Magadha and defeated them.'

'Yes, My Lord.'

'Is it true that you are holding Ajatsattu captive?' asked the Buddha curiously.

'Yes, My Lord, I have, and you know why.'

'Yes, I do,' the Sakyamuni said. After Pasenadi and his queens washed the feet of the Buddha with scented water, he entered the assembly with his disciples. Seeing the Buddha inside the assembly hall, Ajatsattu bowed reverently at him from a distance. The Buddha and other *bhikkhus* were offered seats.

'Maharaj Pasenadi,' The Awakened One spoke softly but impressively after accepting water and food. 'You have done what any king would have done in your position.' Turning towards Ajatsattu, he said, 'My dear Ajatsattu, your father, the great Bimbisara, was a good friend of mine. He had resorted to the path of *dhamma*, and you had him killed by succumbing to the conspiracy hatched by my cousin, Devadatta. Even earlier under his provocation, you had attempted to kill me with an irate elephant. By your wrongful actions, you became the king of the great kingdom of Magadha. But right now, as a consequence of your greed for the throne of Magadha, and for your bad *kamma*s, your army is defeated and you are now held captive as a prisoner.'

Ajatsattu kept sitting with his head held down and gave no response to Tathagata's assertion.

'O Master, please advise me my course of action for Ajatsattu,' requested Pasenadi.

'Maharaj, Ajatsattu's act of imprisoning his father Bimbisara and letting him die in captivity, which resulted in the death of your sister, the Maharani of Magadha, is definitely reprehensible. As a consequence of his bad *kamma*s, he has been defeated in the battle against you and now suffers the humiliation of being held as a captive despite being a king,' the Buddha said calmly. Looking straight into Pasenadi's eyes, he continued, 'Maharaj, I recommend you to liberate Ajatsattu from your imprisonment and reinstate his kingdom.'

'But, My Lord ... ' Pasenadi looked perplexed and could say nothing. A clamour arose in the assembly. There were many who did not adhere to Buddha's *dhamma*, but no one dared to speak against him. Pasenadi beckoned his advisors to come close for discussion, while the people in the court waited with bated breath. Ajatsattu sat restlessly, fixing his gaze at the Buddha, who, along with his disciples, went into deep meditation. Vajira and Vidudabha whispered to one another, wondering what would happen next.

After some time, the courtier declared, 'Listen, the people of Savathi. Listen, Ajatsattu, the captive of Magadha. Upholding the words of the most loved and revered Tathagata, the great King Pasenadi is hereby returning the kingdom of Magadha to Ajatsattu.' Taking a deep breath, the announcer continued, 'Ajatsattu, you who have been detained as a prisoner are being set free to become the Maharaj of Magadha once again.'

***

Ajatsattu, who was listening to the announcer in self-conscious innocence, appeared relaxed after the pronouncement. His glance shifted to Pasenadi, who was waiting impatiently for the Buddha to arise from his dhyana. Slowly, Tathagata opened his eyes and his gaze was unexpectedly set on Vajira.

'Is that your daughter from your chief queen, O, Maharaj Pasenadi?' asked Tathagata.

Pasenadi turned to see his daughter standing with Vidudabha.

'Yes, Master,' answered Pasenadi. Vajira had bloomed into a beautiful girl and her parents desired to marry her off to a good prince of a *mahajanapada*, who subsequently would be crowned the king of that kingdom.

'Maharaj, now that you have honoured Ajatsattu, the son of my deceased friend Bimbisara, by returning his kingdom, let this memorable moment be witness to a happy wedlock.'

'How is that to be done, My Lord?' questioned Pasenadi.

'It is my desire that your daughter Vajira be wedded to Maharaj Ajatsattu of Magadha,' the Buddha replied, closing his eyes. Again, there was a ruckus in the large hall. No one was prepared for such a decision, neither Pasenadi nor Mallika, neither Ajatsattu nor Vajira. But if the verdict came from the Buddha, it could not have been shunned. Pasenadi looked at Mallika; she closed her eyes, gesturing compliance with the Buddha's resolution.

'As you desire, My Lord,' declared Maharaja Pasenadi.

'This matrimony would cement a relationship for the betterment of both Kosala and Magadha.' A silence descended in the assembly as Pasenadi and his two queens retreated to the inner quarters to discuss Buddha's directive of the marriage. After a brief deliberation, the three agreed to the proposal of the Buddha. Returning to the assembly, Pasenadi turned to Ajatsattu.

'Does the Maharaj of Magadha have anything to say to Tathagata's proposition of your marriage to Rajkumari Vajira?' asked Pasenadi.

'The Venerated One's wish is my own,' answered Ajatsattu, speaking after a long time. His roving eyes searched for Vajira, who he found was standing beside a large pillar along with a young boy looking at him. She, at once, lowered her eyes.

Eventually, it was decided to marry off Vajira to Ajatsattu in about a fortnight's time. Until then, he was to stay in the palace as a royal guest of the king.

Chellana and Khema, both stepmothers of Ajatsattu, were also brought to Savathi with honour.

Small channels flow noisily; the great flow silent.
Whatever's not full makes noise. Whatever is full is quiet.

—Sutta Nipata

One morning, when Maharaja Ajatsattu was engaged in a game of swords with a few warriors of Kosala, Vidudabha walked in. Seeing his to-be brother-in-law, Ajatsattu signalled his opponent to stop.

'You must be Prince Vidudabha, the future king of Kosala,' smiled Ajatsattu and lowered his sword.

Vidudabha nodded.

'Young Sir, do you like sword fights?' asked Ajatsattu.

'Yes, I do,' replied Vidudabha.

'You would know that your sister and I are getting married and that she will travel to Rajagaha with me. Would you like to accompany your sister to Rajagaha, Yuvraj?'

'Really? That would be fun, but I shall have to ask my parents,' Vidudabha said with great excitement.

'Surely, you must.'

'Do you have a very large army? I love war.'

'Yes, I do. Well, may be not as strong as your father's, but still is large enough. My dear Yuvraj, if you accompany us to Rajagaha, you can see our soldiers practice. I shall see that you get some sword-fighting lessons and be a witness to some wrestling bouts too. The Magadhas are great wrestlers, you know.'

***

Vajira was wedded to Ajatsattu on the allotted auspicious day, and subsequently left for Rajagaha with her husband amidst much fanfare. Both the queen mothers, Mallika and Vasabhakhatiya, Vajira's maternal grandparents, and various other relatives bade her farewell in tears.

Maharaja Pasenadi was also teary-eyed. Young Vidudabha accompanied his sister and brother-in-law to Rajagaha. This being his first journey outside Savathi without his mother, he felt a little ill at ease despite being in high spirits. He sat in the royal palanquin along with his didi Vajira, who was now the maharani of Magadha. Vasabhakhatiya had sent Vidudabha's Brahmin tutor along with him so that his studies were not neglected in all the fun.

***

Rajagaha was soon drowned in celebrations. Music from drums and wind instruments resonated from every corner of the capital. The citizens, who were deeply pained on losing their favourite king Bimbisara and queen Kosala Devi, put aside their misery by welcoming the new maharani Vajira.

Rajagaha became a place of illimitable fun for Vidudabha, as he indulged in merriment with the boys of the palace. Ajatsattu had assigned two attendants at the prince's service. 'This young man is my brother-in-law and also the Yuvraj of Kosala. See that he has everything,' the king instructed his attendants. 'Take him to see the practice sessions of our warriors and to the wresting *akhadas* as well.' Wrestling was Magadha's main sport and the *mahajanapada* was famous for its wrestlers. With both Bimbisara and Ajatsattu being skilled wrestlers, the sport had received a fillip under them.

'I cannot wait to see those big wrestlers,' Vidudabha leaped with joy. *Kushti* bouts were specially arranged for him, as he had never witnessed one but only heard of them.

Vidudabha's education continued even in Rajagaha, as the Brahmin teacher who had accompanied the prince from Savathi tutored him both in the morning and the evening. One day, after his studies, Vidudabha went to take a look at the sword fight. Trained swordsmen were displaying their skills when Maharaja Ajatsattu, without prior notice, entered the ring.

'Come Yuvraj, let's fight,' Ajatsattu extended an invitation to Vidudabha with a challenging smile. Vidudabha returned the smile to his brother-in-law and leaped into the arena with great vigour. The prince was offered a sword, and the unusual duel between the king and the young prince kicked off.

Maharaja Ajatsattu and the Magadha soldiers were indeed astounded to find the young prince of Kosala proficient and accomplished in the combat. The young prince seemed to know many tactics of the sport. Although Ajatsattu emerged victorious, he indeed was full of praises for his young brother-in-law.

'You are such a good fighter, Yuvraj. From whom do you receive your training?' asked Ajatsattu.

'Well, our Senapati Digha Karayana teaches me.'

'He is a very good tutor, Yuvraj, and he is training you adequately. By the time you come of my age, you will certainly become the most skilled swordsman of this region,' prophesized Maharaja Ajatsattu, patting his back. 'Are you good in archery too?'

'Why don't you test me, Maharaj?'

'I admire your poise, Young Prince. Alright, we shall see that tomorrow before I leave for Videha later in the day,' said the king.

'I shall also ask your didi, the Maharani, to witness your deftness in archery tomorrow. Will that be fine, Yuvraj?'

'My didi knows nothing about my skills,' replied Vidudabha with a smile.

Next morning, both Maharaja Ajatsattu and his newly wedded wife Maharani Vajira walked with Vidudabha to the archery ground. 'I have never seen your prowess in archery, Viru. Heard that Maharaj was highly impressed with your sword fight,' quipped Vajira.

'Well, may be. But, Didi, do see for yourself.'

Vidudabha touched the feet of his elder sister and brother-in-law respectfully before running to the archery field. Vidudabha's targets were four moderate-sized pumpkins hung from a *mahua* tree at a distance.

'This is quite close. I'd rather stand at a greater distance,' Vidudabha's voice disclosed much confidence.

'I love the young man's attitude,' Ajatsattu said to his queen smilingly. After Vidudabha had moved a little further away from his designated location, an attendant gave him a bow and a quiver with a few arrows. Fixing his arrow to the sling of the bow, Vidudabha concentrated on his targets before shooting. In no time, all the four pumpkins were smashed by Vidudabha's arrows, astonishing both the maharaja, the maharani, and the other onlookers.

'Excellent, Young Prince!' everyone exclaimed in unison. Vajira looked at her brother with admiration and pride.

***

The following night, when Ajatsattu returned from Videha, Vidudabha confided in him that although he was receiving his weapons' training under the senapati of Kosala, he nurtured a firm desire to be trained by his maternal grandfather Mahanama in Kapilavatthu, who was renowned as a celebrated archer.

'Indeed, it is widely known that your grandfather Mahanama is the finest archer in the world,' Ajatsattu agreed.

***

Eventually, after his stay in Rajagaha for over three months, Vidudabha left for Savathi, enriching himself with experiences in various combats. With moist eyes, Vajira bade goodbye to her brother, while Ajatsattu took Vidudabha's promise that he would visit Magadha soon and stay for a longer time.

All forms of existence are unreal (an-atta); he who perceives the truth of this gets disgusted with this world of suffering.

—Dhammapada

Returning from Rajagaha, Rajkumar Vidudabha conveyed to his mother that he desires to be trained in archery by his grandfather Mahanama in Kapilavatthu. He revealed that from his childhood, he had been secretly nurturing an ambition to become a proficient archer like Ekalavya and Arjuna. He had heard countless tales about his grandfather Mahanama's archery skills. He insisted that he be allowed to travel to Kapilavatthu to hone his skills in archery from his grandfather.

Vidudabha's constant badgering became a worrisome issue for Vasabhakhatiya. She feared that the truth about her not being a princess but the daughter of a *dasi* of Mahanama, which she had been keeping from her husband and her son, and, in fact, from everyone in Kosala, lay there in Kapilavatthu. This truth had to be kept from everybody, or else she would face a devastating consequence. When Vidudabha was a baby, Vasabhakhatiya did visit her mother in Kapilavatthu a couple of times, but now that the prince was grown-up, he had to be intercepted from visiting there so that the truth remained a secret. But could she really do it? It is said that no matter how skilfully the truth is concealed, it has the bad habit of revealing itself.

'Not now, Son,' Vasabhakhatiya somehow resisted.

'No, Mai, I shall have to go. I cannot wait any further,' Vidudabha was adamant.

'Digha is already training you in archery, sword fights, and other combats, is he not? So what is the need for you to go to your grandfather?' Vasabhakhatiya tried hard to prevent her son from travelling to Kapilavatthu.

'True Mai, but Grandfather is the best in this sport and learning from him would be a greater prestige.'

'It may take months, or may be a few years for the training, my boy. How can I live without you for so long?'

'Mai, you could come and visit me in between,' Vidudabha said. Then, pausing for a while, he asserted, 'I learn from Grandfather or no one else. That is my final decision.' Saying this, young Vidudabha stormed out of the room, leaving his mother in trepidation and entirely helpless. Her face coloured deeply and then waned. She knew that her son must have gone straight to his father in his royal chamber.

The king was getting ready to leave for his assembly when Vidudabha walked in abruptly.

'My Yuvraj, have you finally remembered your father?' Pasenadi smiled at his son.

'Baba, I have something to tell you,' Vidudabha came straight to the matter.

'Yes, Prince, but first tell me how are your studies going?'

'Fine, Father.'

'Good. Next year, you shall go to the University of Takshashila for higher education, the place where I went. What about your weaponry?'

'It is about that, Father.'

'Go ahead, Son.'

'I wish to go to Kapilavatthu to be trained in archery by my grandfather Mahanama,' said Vidudabha.

'What a brilliant idea! Your grandfather Mahanama is indeed a great warrior and the greatest archer of our times. Learning from him ... it never occurred to me. You must go, Son.'

'Thank you, Maharaj.'

'When do you wish to leave, Yuvraj?'

'Whenever you command, Father.'

'Next week, maybe. But have you sought permission from your queen mothers?' asked Pasenadi.

'My mother doesn't want me to go to Kapilavatthu. She wants me to continue my training under Senapati,' answered Vidudabha.

'Ha, ha. Actually, my boy, no mother would want to be separated from her young lad for so long. But then, you are the future king of Kosala. Petty sentiments should have no place in your life. I shall speak to her. You prepare to depart for Kapilavatthu. Digha would also accompany you to the kingdom of the Sakyas,' Pasenadi patted on his son's shoulders and walked out of his room for his assembly.

***

Standing at the far end of the inner door, Vasabhakhatiya eavesdropped on the father–son tête-à-tête. Sensing the looming tempest in their lives, her heart pounded so loud she could almost hear it. She shuddered to think of the outcome when her husband, Maharaja Pasenadi, gets to discover that she, in actuality, is a *dasi-putri* who was coerced by her father and the other Sakya officials to disguise as a Sakya princess to marry him.

The queen, escorted by one of her female attendants, slipped out of the palace incognito and went to the mango grove. She had already sent news to Punna, her personal errand man, to meet her at the grove. He arrived in some time.

'Yes, Rani Mai,' pleaded Punna.

'I have summoned you for an assignment of utmost significance,' Vasabhakhatiya replied.

'Order me, O, Queen.'

'But prior to that, you should promise me that you will not speak to anyone about this rendezvous, not even to the king,' Vasabhakhatiya said firmly, looking straight into Punna's eyes.

'You have my word for it, Rani Mai,' assured Punna.

'Good. Carry my message to the Nayaka of Kapilavatthu.'

'Yes, Your Highness.'

'Here, take this. You shall deliver this to Nayaka Mahanama,' saying this, Vasabhakhatiya produced a small, sealed satchel, red in colour, from under her wrapper and handed it to Punna. 'After you deliver this to the Raja, collect what he provides you with and then return immediately to Savathi and give it to me.'

'Yes, your Highness,' Punna bowed in silence.

'Alright then, depart right now for Kapilavatthu.'

Without wasting further time, Punna left.

***

Once in Kapilavatthu, Punna delivered the message to Mahanama. The satchel was opened by the raja himself, who found a small *bhojpatra* inside on which Vasabhakhatiya had written, 'Vidudabha will arrive at Kapilavatthu next week. He wishes to learn archery from his grandfather Mahanama, for which he would stay there for long. I remain incapable to stop him from travelling to Kapilavatthu.'

Though short, the message was adequate enough for Mahanama to foresee the impending crisis.

The mind, when undeveloped, leads to great harm.

—Akammaniya Vagga

It had been pouring all night long, but by morning the rains abated. The sky was still a gloomy grey and overcast. The palace hummed with activity as the prince prepared to set off for Kapilavatthu, the land of his mother and his maternal grandparents. Senapati Digha Karayana, along with a small band of soldiers, was to accompany Vidudabha to Kapilavatthu. While two sentries would stay on to attend to the yuvraj, the senapati would return the next day.

Bidding farewell to his father Maharaja Pasenadi, Maharani Mallika, the elderly women of the palace, and to his friends, young Vidudabha mounted his horse. His probing eyes scanned the palace for his mother, whom he found peering at him from the upper-floor window. He had already touched her feet before wishing goodbye. Vidudabha and his soldiers, along with Senapati Digha, embarked on their three-day long journey to Kapilavatthu. Vasabhakhatiya saw her son riding into the realm of her past, an act she knew was to overturn everything in her present.

She receded to her shrine room, where she lay prostrate in front of the sacred stones that she worshipped as Abhaya Devi and Sin Bonga. Little did she know that even the gods were incapable of stalling the upshot of bad *kamma*s that were initiated a few years ago.

***

'Senapati, Baba has told me that as the rains are here, Tathagata and his *sangha* may have arrived at Jethavan. He has directed that we need to halt there and take his blessings before moving further,' said Vidudabha.

'Sure, Dear Prince,' replied Digha.

The road was wet and so were the trees. Very soon, they arrived at Jethavan. There were a few brick structures created for the accommodation and prayers of the *bhikkhus*. A group of orange-robed monks sat meditating on one such brick platform under a large mango tree. The prince's entourage observed an orange-robe-clad old man sitting in deep dhyana in the *padmasana* posture below a dense peepal tree. Vidudabha and his people recognized him to be the The Enlightened One, the Buddha. All alighted from their horses silently, lest they disturb the meditating monks. Settling quietly on the moistened ground at a little distance from the meditating Buddha, they waited for him to open his eyes. Shortly, the Buddha came out of his dhyana to find Vidudabha and his men waiting patiently for him. The rajkumar rose to kiss his lotus feet, and the Buddha showered *abhayadan* and blessed them all. 'Yuvraj, where are you going this morning?' the Buddha's wrinkled face glowed with a tender smile.

'We are travelling to your homeland, O Master, which incidentally is also the land of my mother. I intend to learn archery from my grandfather, Nayaka Mahanama. Father has instructed me to take your blessings before I leave Savathi,' Vidudabha replied.

'That is good, my boy. Mahanama, as I know, is certainly a skilled archer. Young lad, ride carefully. I, too, shall be going to Kapilavatthu in a few days.'

The convoy then resumed its journey.

Kasyapa, who stood a little far away, was listening to Vidudabha converse with the Buddha. He said now, 'The Rajkumar seems quite straightforward and candid, O Master.'

'Straight trees, my dear Kasyapa, may look sturdy, but they break easily. The problem I sense with Vidudabha is that he has great patience, but possesses a dormant violent temper, a combination that is undeniably lethal,' Tathagata replied after a short pause.

I say categorically, Ananda, that bodily misconduct, verbal misconduct, and mental misconduct should not be done.

—Ekamsena Sutta

It was already past noon when Vidudabha and his men reached Kapilavatthu, weary and hungry after a journey that spanned two nights and about three days. Though a messenger from Maharaja Pasenadi had been despatched to Kapilavatthu earlier to notify the arrival of Vidudabha, the yuvraj of Kosala and the grandson of Mahanama, no welcoming party was there to receive him.

'This is humiliating. The Sakyas were informed about our arrival in advance, yet no one is here to greet the prince,' remarked Digha surprisingly.

'What should we do now, Senapati?' asked the young prince.

'Honourable Kumar, I believe we should first go to their *santhagara*, where the council sits headed by your grandfather, the Nayaka,' replied Digha.

The townspeople gazed at the small procession of the young prince and his soldiers heading for the *santhagara*. Arriving there, Digha signalled his soldiers to halt and advised Vidudabha to wait, while he sent two of his soldiers to enter the *santhagara* and inform Mahanama of the rajkumar's arrival.

The soldiers were permitted to go inside the *sabha kuti* of the *santhagara*, where a meeting of the *amala*s headed by Mahanama was in progress. The soldiers announced the arrival of the grandson of the raja of Kapilavatthu, hearing which people started talking in hushed voices. Mahanama instructed an attendant to accompany the Kosala soldiers and fetch the prince. Digha entered a room next to the *sabha kuti* with the prince, where a heated discussion continued amongst the men, unmindful of the prince's arrival. The guests were made to sit on a large *chatai* in the next room.

At length, when the meeting concluded, both the yuvraj and the senapati were ushered inside the *sabha kuti*. There, on an elevated platform, sat Mahanama. Vidudabha respectfully touched the feet of his grandfather.

'Welcome to Kapilavatthu, Yuvraj,' said Mahanama. 'I hope you had a pleasant journey.'

'Yes, Sir,' said Vidudabha.

'Trust your parents are well?' enquired Mahanama.

'Yes, they are, and they offer their respects to you.'

Mahanama nodded grimly in reply.

'These are the elected members of the *ganarajya* of Kapilavatthu,' Mahanama said, indicating his council members.

Vidudabha conveyed his *johar* to the councillors of the Sakya *ganarajya* by bowing to them, but oddly, no one acknowledged him. He then went to the councillors in the front row to touch their feet. 'Stay there, no need to come closer,' old Harita asked Vidudabha to stop, while another spat on the floor looking at the prince.

'Kosala Senapati, you may leave now and take your prince away too,' Bhalatiya directed Digha. The senapati found the behaviour of the councillors towards the rajkumar derogatory and disrespectful, given the fact that Kosala was one of the strongest kingdoms and its king Maharaja Pasenadi and his father Mahakosala (incidentally, he was Mahanama's friend too) were among the most powerful kings of all times. He wondered at the strange behaviour of the *amala*s towards Vidudabha. His instincts cautioned him that some unfair play was transpiring here of which he knew nothing. The senapati made up his mind to get to the root of this riddle.

The contingent that accompanied Vidudabha was still not asked of water and food. Digha knew that both the soldiers and their horses outside must be famished.

'Respected Nayaka, isn't it strange that your members of the *sangha* did not greet our Prince? Is it because he is young, or do you desire to humiliate Kosala?' Digha asked Mahanama, who was busy conversing with a few of his *amalas*.

'Oh no, Senapati, please do not think so. Actually, Siddhartha will be arriving here in a few days. This meeting is in that regard. We are discussing about how to welcome him at Kapilavatthu. Perhaps, in this stress, my men may have behaved a little inelegantly towards the Yuvraj,' replied Mahanama softly. Mahanama's kind words did not, however, convince Digha.

'I presume, Sir, that you would know the reason for our young Yuvraj's arrival.'

'Yes, I do. He wishes to learn archery from me, does he not? He shall stay here for a long time.'

'Yes, Sir. And now, it would be nice if you could ask your men to arrange shelter for our Prince, and food and water for us and our horses,' Digha made it clear.

'Ah yes, I forgot. Rajkumar Vidudabha will stay at my guest house. The rest of you will stay in the *ganasangha*'s guest house. Food will be served to you, and your horses will be taken care of. My men will look after things,' saying this, Mahanama instructed his men to make all arrangements.

'I leave tomorrow, but Maharaj Pasenadi has commanded me to be with the Prince till then,' Digha informed Mahanama.

'In that case, Senapati, you may stay with your Prince tonight.'

The world is a place of suffering (dukkha). Suffering is everywhere. Dukkha should be understood.

—The First Noble Truth

Late afternoon.

Vidudabha was sleeping in the guest house after a sumptuous lunch, when the door opened and Nagamunda, the prince's grandmother, and her attendant entered the room. Nagamunda was now an elderly lady, and she looked dark as the night.

Around the same time, Digha too ambled into the room. He was amazed to see the two women advancing towards the sleeping yuvraj. The senapati stopped them.

'Ladies, what is it that you want from my Rajkumar? Can't you see that he is resting?' Digha asked.

'She is the grandmother of your Rajkumar,' the female attendant replied, pointing towards Nagamunda.

'Oh! What a privilege, Your Highness.'

The din in the room awakened Vidudabha, who rose up and sat on the bed. Nagamunda fixed her gaze on her grandson. Clasping his face with both her palms, she kissed his temple and softly muttered, 'My boy, how you have grown! You look just like your mother. You would not remember me now, but as a kid you used to play on my lap during your visits here.' Vidudabha gaped with awe. 'My boy, I am your grandmother,' said Nagamunda, caressing his face.

Vidudabha gazed at her for a while and then touched her feet with deep reverence. Nagamunda held him close to her bosom as tears rolled down her cheeks.

'You are my Vasu's son. Never did I imagine that I would be able to see you again,' Nagamunda confessed to Vidudabha, holding him close. At that moment, the front door opened and Mahanama entered. Beholding the loving sight, he smiled. Vidudabha bowed to his grandfather.

'Vidudabha, this will be your home as long as you are in Kapilavatthu,' said the nayaka.

'When shall we begin our training, Sir?' asked Vidudabha.

'Very soon. You will be informed.'

'I learnt that I have a few cousins. Where are they, Sir?' Vidudabha asked his grandfather.

'They have gone out on a picnic and will perhaps return late in the night,' replied Mahanama.

'Did they not know that I was to come today?'

'Why is it necessary for them to know it?' There was a sudden annoyance in Mahanama's voice as his face suddenly turned stiff. He added, 'Now listen, Vidudabha, you are here to learn archery from me. Hence, you shall stay away from your cousins and concentrate on your training.' Mahanama spoke very harshly as he walked out of the house, ordering Nagamunda to depart from there at the earliest.

Nagamunda looked at her grandson with moist eyes and placed a kiss on his forehead. Then she rushed briskly out of the house, followed by her attendant. Both Digha and Vidudabha were left nonplussed.

The Kosala senapati regarded Mahanama's behaviour towards the young prince abysmal, as well as an insult targeted at the kingdom of Kosala. Although Vidudabha was young, he could understand that his grandfather's behaviour towards him was offensive, and that hurt him deeply. He wondered as to why his cousins did not wait for him to arrive from Savathi so that he could join them for the picnic. Vidudabha might not be able to meet them any more, as his grandfather had firmly instructed him to focus on archery and to stay away from his cousins.

But why? Digha wondered too.

***

In the early hours of the next day, as Digha snored away, Vidudabha went for a stroll on the streets of Kapilavatthu. The streets were largely empty in the rain-soaked morning, except for a handful of women gathered near the wells for drawing water and a few men carrying their ploughs to the fields. Some cows, buffaloes, goats, pigs, and dogs meandered indolently in the roads. Looking around lazily, Vidudabha arrived at an open field where he spotted a few children playing *chua-chui*, one of his favourite games, on a newly constructed platform. Walking towards the pulpit, he stood watching them when one of the young girls called him, 'Come up and join us.'

At first, Vidudabha remained silent as he was older than the kids. But soon, hesitatingly, he climbed up the steps of the platform.

'Are you new to this place?' one of the boys asked.

'Yes, I am. I live in Savathi,' replied Vidudabha. He then joined in the game.

No sooner had a few moments passed than a thundering voice had the children stop the game. 'How dare this low-born boy get on the platform meant for Tathagata? Get down immediately, you! Yes, you, the one from Savathi!' It was his grandfather Mahanama who, while returning from his morning yoga, found his grandson playing on the podium built for Tathagata, who was to arrive here in a few days.

'How can you, the son of a slave woman's daughter, get up on this sacred platform meant for the Buddha and pollute it! Go away immediately and never come back here!' Mahanama spit venom at his grandson in a fit of rage. Young Vidudabha, in inconceivable shock, rushed down from the podium and stood aside, quivering like a leaf on a windy day. Noticing Mahanama standing beside the platform, people scampered out of their homes.

'Listen, all of you. Tathagata is arriving here in a day or two. You all know that this platform has been built for him,' the raja announced in an assertive voice. Everyone nodded. Mahanama continued, 'This boy here is the grandson of a *dasi*. By ascending this holy podium, the boy has polluted it. I want you people to purify it by cleansing the platform with cow dung and the holy water of the Rohini. Also see that no low caste, as this boy, steps on the podium henceforth. Is that clear to all?'

'Yes, Mahanayaka,' everyone replied in unison. Then, turning towards Vidudabha, the men yelled, 'Go away, you! Off you go! How dare you come here to play with our children? Get off with you!'

Who knows the path of peace: let them be able and upright, straightforward and gentle in speech, humble and not conceited, contented and easily satisfied.

—Karaniya Metta Sutta

Vidudabha trudged back, dejected.

The prince had never faced such humiliation in front of so many people. He felt like some kind of a pariah dog banished with hatred by his own grandfather. An urge to scream aloud took hold of him as tears streamed down his cheeks.

And what gibberish was his grandfather uttering? That he was the grandson of a slave woman, huh?

He suddenly stopped in his tracks.

What if this was really true?

Vidudabha slowly walked into the guest house. Digha and his soldiers surrounded the prince as soon as they saw him walk in with teary eyes and a gloomy countenance. Recovering gradually from the shock, the prince recounted the harrowing incident to his men. The soldiers immediately pulled out their swords from their scabbards. 'How dare they insult our Rajkumar! We shall chop off the old fellow's head.'

Digha raised his hands to placate his soldiers. He knew that Vidudabha was being slighted since the time they arrived at Kapilavatthu. Digha understood that there ought to be some iota of truth behind the reprimands. He wondered whether the dark woman who claimed to be the prince's grandmother yesterday was the slave woman in question.

Digha could now sense that all these infuriating incidents occurring at Kapilavatthu surely hinted at a conspiracy against Kosala and Maharaja Pasenadi. The scheme may have been devised some time in the past that had something to do with Mahanama, Nagamunda, Vidudabha, and a few others; some involved on purpose and some inadvertently. He had to get to the source of this.

At that moment, the door opened and two cleaning women entered with pitchers at their sides.

'We need to clean the room. Could you please wait outside as we sweep and wipe the floor?' All of them walked out, but Digha stood behind the door to eavesdrop on the conversation happening between the two women. What if, by any chance, they talk about Vidudabha's identity? Vidudabha too stood beside the senapati. Digha gestured him to listen silently.

'Wipe and clean every bit of the floor. We do not know where he would have walked around in the room,' Digha and Vidudabha overheard the elderly cleaning woman speaking to the younger one. The prying men could not clearly grasp their conversation, although Digha realized that something was indeed the matter.

Young Vidudabha was able to comprehend that it was he whom the Sakyas believed was polluting every place. All the tantrums, abuses, and embarrassments were directed at him. He recalled how Mahanama was enraged on finding him on the podium and how he indicted him of contaminating it just by being there. And now these women were purifying his room by cleaning it thoroughly, as his presence had supposedly tainted it.

At this point, Digha suddenly opened the door and walked into the room.

'Do you know who we are?' Digha unswervingly questioned the matured one.

'Yes Sir, he is the Yuvraj of Kosala and you are the Senapati.'

'Tell me, what is this talk about polluting this room? Who is polluting it?' Digha asked. But the women continued with their work silently.

'Speak up!' commanded Digha.

'Do you not know, Sir?' one of them asked feebly.

'No, I don't. I would not have asked had I known, isn't it? Now tell us.'

Both the women stopped working and looked at one another.

'Sir, we are poor, working women. If the *amalas* come to know that we have disclosed the truth to you, we could be punished,' the elderly woman spoke up.

'Be assured, woman, that your names will never be uttered. Besides, we do not even know your names. Speak up now,' instructed Digha authoritatively.

'Sir, we believe that the Rajkumar here is polluting everything, as he is of low birth.'

'Low birth? But how? Isn't he the grandchild of Mahanama, the Raja of Kapilavatthu, and his mother the Princess of your kingdom?' queried a stunned Digha.

'Sir, Vasabhakhatiya is not the Princess of Kapilavatthu. Her mother is the slave of Raja Mahanama, and hence the Yuvraj here is a son of a *dasi-putri*. Nagamunda, the woman who came to see him yesterday, is the *dasi*. Being the son of a *dasi-putri*, is he not of low origin? Will his presence not contaminate every place, including this room?'

Vidudabha and Digha stood gaping at the women in shock. The cleaning women divulged more untold secrets. It was, of course, known that Pasenadi desired to marry a Sakya princess. But what was not known was that the Kosalas were considered lowly born by the Sakyas. For this reason, Mahanama and the council had refused to send a real Sakya princess for the marriage. But afraid that the denial could result in an attack on Kapilavatthu by Maharaja Pasenadi, the slave woman Nagamunda's daughter Vasabhakhatiya was sent to Savathi by Mahanama and the council of Kapilavatthu, faking her as the *ganarajya*'s princess. The marriage was formalized and Prince Vidudabha was born of it. As the *dasi-putri*'s son, Vidudabha was despised by all here.

This disclosure left both Vidudabha and Digha astounded and speechless. After what Pasenadi had done to his uncle Bandhula and his cousins, Digha was thrilled on sensing the suffering that the maharaja will will go through after learning of his deceitful marriage. Digha remembered the Buddha's saying that bad *kamma* always has a bad consequence.

All of a sudden, the sound of stones being pelted at the guest house was heard. Digha opened the door and walked out to find a number of Sakyas congregated outside the house.

'Why are you all stoning the house?' asked the senapati.

'Get that low-born boy out of here! He had the audacity to play with our children and even impure the platform meant for Tathagata,' one of the Sakyas retorted.

'Do you not know that he is the Rajkumar of Kosala?'

'We do not care who he may be. We only know that he is the grandson of a *dasi* and he cannot stay at a place meant for "pure" people; he should have put up somewhere in the city fringes. Get him out of Nayaka Mahanama's guest house.'

'Alright, we shall leave very soon. But first, move away from here or else my anger can get the better of you all.'

There never existed, nor will there ever exist, nor does there exist today anyone who is always scorned or always praised.

—Dhammapada

Returning inside, Digha found Vidudabha standing as if turned to stone. He looked troubled and his temple gleamed with beads of perspiration. The senapati could make out that a storm was raging in the dejected heart of the young yuvraj. Before long, Vidudabha unexpectedly broke down into tears.

'I feel like a tiny insect,' Vidudabha dropped on his bed and, covering his face, sobbed relentlessly. 'All this time, my mai knew who I was, and yet she kept both the king and me in the dark. Why?' he lamented, raising his face.

'Honourable Kumar, do not blame the poor Rani Mai. As her son, try to understand her pain and misery. Do you not see that she was merely a pawn in this dirty game played by the wicked Mahanama and his *amalas*?' explained Digha.

'You are right, Senapati. But I can also see that my life is devastated due to Mahanama and the Sakyas. Here in Kapilavatthu, I am the victim of constant slur, perhaps enough to last my lifetime,' Vidudabha said softly yet firmly. 'Their wrong against my mother, my grandmother, and me cannot go unheeded. They must pay for their sins.' There was an underlying belligerence in the young prince's voice, as if the words did not emanate from the juvenile Vidudabha but from a calm, thoughtful, and level-headed person. The senapati gaped at the prince, dumbfounded and befuddled.

Strains of melodies by rowing boatmen on the distant Rohini soared into the room through the open window. Vidudabha gazed through the window at the serene view of the sailing boats on the Rohini far away. Digha could sense the torment that the young rajkumar was undergoing, but there wasn't anything he could do to help him ease his pain.

'Senapati, when I become the king of Kosala, I shall make each and every Sakya pay for their crime,' said Vidudabha, as he kept looking at the river in the distance.

'Kumar, your words scare me. The turn of events here seem to have affected you greatly.'

'It has, Senapati,' Vidudabha replied after a while.

'My Prince, being elder to you, I would advise you to return home at the earliest and forget Kapilavatthu forever, or else these unpleasant incidents would keep eating at you.'

'No, Senapati, I cannot forget Kapilavatthu ever. But I shall see that the world forgets it,' Vidudabha said self-assuredly.

'I may be young, O Senapati, but still old enough to understand that Mahanama has ruined both my mother's and my life. I shall never forget the abuses my maternal grandfather and his Sakyas have hurled at me,' Vidudabha said compellingly. 'Senapati, today in Kapilavatthu, I pledge that I shall slaughter Mahanama along with each Sakya for the pains he and his people have caused to my mother, my grandmother, and to me. I shall erase Kapilavatthu from the face of this earth, forever.'

The cold and resentful proclamation of Vidudabha had Digha Karayana look anxiously into the prince's determined eyes. An unknown chill ran down the senapati's spine, sending a tremor through him.

The world is afflicted by death and decay. But the wise do not grieve, having realized the nature of the world.

—Sutta Nipata

'Summon Rani Vasabhakhatiya,' roared Pasenadi. His anger was apparent from the beads of sweat and the deep lines on his tense forehead, after his son and senapati relayed the hidden secret of how the maharaja had been duped into marrying Vasabhakhatiya.

Standing behind the assembly door and listening to her son's unpleasant encounter in Kapilavatthu, Vasabhakhatiya was trembling in utter dread. She eventually appeared silently at the call of her husband, the maharaja of Kosala. The mere sight of his wife had Pasenadi explode into such a rage that words failed to escape his mouth. His lips trembled with uncontrollable anger.

'Kosala has been cheated,' declared the king after regaining control of his faculties. 'I have been tricked by the Sakyas and even by her,' Pasenadi pointed at Vasabhakhatiya, whose eyes did not shed a drop of tear. She stood there petrified, her head drooping.

'Vasabhakhatiya, the Rani of Kosala, is the daughter of a *dasi*! They tricked me into marrying a slave woman's daughter! Tch, tch, tch! It seems that I am already a laughing stock among the people of my own country, in Kapilavatthu, and in the entire world. How deviously the Raja of Kapilavatthu hoodwinked me into marrying a slave woman's daughter feigning her as the ganarajya's Princess. How humiliating! I allowed this slave woman's girl to be my queen, and she delivered the future king of Kosala! Our great Kosala has been cheated by her, by her father Mahanama, and by her people,' thundered the king.

An uncomfortable silence prevailed in the court of Savathi as the fidgety hands of Maharaja Pasenadi kept rubbing his bald head and face in utter restiveness.

'No, this can't be ... this cannot go unpunished!' declared Pasenadi. 'Minister!' he yelled. 'Order your men to arrest Rani Vasabhakhatiya and her son Vidudabha. If they belong to the slave family, let it be so. Take them away to the slave quarters and make sure that they are treated not as rani and rajkumar but as slaves. Also see that they are made to toil as slaves. Go, take them away from my sight ... go!'

It was as if a lightning had struck the assembly, turning everyone into stone. Never had they witnessed such a shocking incident, nor had they even heard of it—a king ordering his own queen and prince to be taken as *dasas*! Even Vidudabha and his mother Vasabhakhatiya froze on hearing the king's orders.

'Father, I am your son and she your wife,' pleaded young Vidudabha, falling on his knees. Tears streamed down the eyes of the beholders. Only Digha stood still and restrained himself to not let his emotions overpower him, for he knew that Maharaja Pasenadi would have to pay dearly for this injustice against his queen and son.

Two guards came forward and silently stood by Vidudabha and Vasabhakhatiya. The queen and the prince did not wait for the sentries to escort them. Instead, they slowly walked out of the assembly themselves with the guards trailing them reluctantly.

Vasabhakhatiya, the maharani of Kosala, now turned into a slave as per the command of her husband, Maharaja Pasenadi. She somehow dragged her cheerless self to the slave quarters. Vidudabha, the young yuvraj of Kosala, who once aspired to become a distinguished archer, was now forced into slavery by his own father. He too made his way despondently to the slave quarters of the palace.

A thump on his shoulder made Vidudabha turn to find Digha looking at him with reassuring eyes.

'Have patience, Kumar,' said Digha softly, as if in a whisper, and nodded his head. After a gentle and reassuring compress on Vidudabha's shoulder, he slowly walked away.

***

Vasabhakhatiya and Vidudabha were allotted separate rooms in the female and male sections of the slave quarters. The segregation between the quarters was intended to be strict as, during nights, the female precinct came alive with shrieks and screams of inebriated men and women that ringed in the night sky. However, the arrival of the queen in the female division did put a check on these activities.

The supervisors were in a perplexity as to how they would order their own queen and prince to perform tasks of slavery, but as the king had cautioned them to show no mercy, they were compelled to allot harsh chores to them, lest they be punished themselves. Storing water in tubs drawn from wells, filling up reservoirs of the palace, lugging firewood for the palace kitchen, weeding the palace lawns, cleaning the stables, bathing the horses and elephants, and even sweeping and wiping the palace chambers where they once lived as the queen and the prince were a few tasks assigned to them. Habituated to palatable drinks and food in the palace, the maharani and rajkumar could not consume the unappetizing food now provided to them.

However many holy words you read, however many you speak, what good will they do if you do not act upon them?

—Dhammapada

On their way to Sarnath, Buddha and Ananda rested in the outskirts of Uruvela, where he had spent a long time attaining Bodhihood or Buddhatva. The *bhikkhus*, during their *pindapatta*, heard about the unfortunate news of the enslavement of Rani Vasabhakhatiya and Yuvraj Vidudabha and the appalling events that led to it. After returning from their rounds, Ananda recounted the incidents to Tathagata. On hearing the accounts, the Buddha closed his eyes and went into deep *vipassana*.

Later, he told Ananda, '*Bhantey*, life is unpredictable and impermanent. All individuals are responsible for the consequences of their own *kammas*. What Mahanama and the Sakyas did to Pasenadi, Vasabhakhatiya, Nagamunda, and Vidudabha was indeed wrong. They will suffer the repercussions of that *kamma* in their own ways.

'Even Pasenadi has wronged. He has punished his wife and son for a crime committed by Mahanama in league with the *amalas*. Everyone shall bear the brunt of their bad *kammas*,' saying this, the Buddha fell silent.

***

The news that Vasabhakhatiya and her son Vidudabha were turned into slaves in their own palace by Pasenadi reached Kapilavatthu.

Nagamunda broke down and wept hysterically, having no one to share her grief with. Later in the day, she walked to the *sarna*, their sacred grove, and conducted rituals by making a *gachti* that she would offer a white cock to Sin Bonga, her deity, if her daughter and grandson were reinstated as the queen and the prince of Kosala. An urgent meeting of the council was convened in the afternoon to discuss the turn of events in Kosala.

'What now, Raja Mahanama?' asked one of the councillors.

'I believe that our behaviour towards Vidudabha, including mine, was indeed appalling. We should have restrained ourselves,' replied Mahanama softly.

'I had always disagreed to your scheme of disguising and sending Vasabhakhatiya as the Princess of Kapilavatthu,' said Bhalatiya.

'What is done cannot be undone. A mistake has been committed by us that requires immediate rectification, or else Pasenadi will raze us to dust,' Mahanama said, biting his lips. 'One of our delegates would soon visit Tathagata to seek solution to this problem. After all, he too is a Sakya.'

'Does anyone know where he is now, O Mahanayaka?' inquired Anantha, one of the councillors.

'He is on his way to Kusinagara from Kashi.'

'Good. We must obtain his suggestion and act accordingly,' said Harita.

Emissaries from various *mahajanapada*s like Gandhara, Anga, Kamboja, Matsya, Panchala, Magadha, and others, as well from several *ganarajyas* like Veshali, Kosambi, Vatsya, and Kolagrama were sent to Maharaja Pasenadi with messages from their respective kings and nayakas to release the rani and the yuvraj from slavery and re-establish their status as before.

Vajira, Pasenadi's daughter, and presently the maharani of Magadha, arrived at Savathi around noon. After reverently touching her father's feet, she said, 'Baba, the ominous state of affairs in Savathi has brought me here.'

'You should not involve yourself in the internal affairs of the state of Kosala, as you are now the Queen of Magadha,' said the king.

'But Baba, I am here as your daughter. The ones whom you have enslaved are my Choti Mai and my loving brother, and their miserable condition distresses me,' replied Vajira.

'My dear girl, they are suffering for their misdeeds. Your Choti Mai concealed her true identity of being a lowly born woman, and thereafter deceitfully had me marry her, while your brother has wronged because he is the son of a *dasi-putri*. They both have betrayed not only me but the people of Kosala. Hence, they have to suffer the punishment.'

'Baba, they have suffered a lot. I earnestly request you to release them now.'

'My dear girl, you have had a long journey. Go inside to your mother.'

Realizing that her father was unbending, she decided to discuss the matter later in the night. She went inside the palace. Once Vajira retreated, Pasenadi asked Sudatta, his minister, 'It seems that punishing the Rani and the Yuvraj has not only turned the kings and the rajas against me, but even my own daughter.'

'I am afraid that is the truth, Maharaj,' responded Sudatta. 'The resentment is quite strong both in Savathi and within our palace.' Pasenadi remembered how Mallika, his chief queen, too, had been incessantly nagging him to free both Vasabhakhatiya and Vidudabha.

'Do you also blame me, Minister?' asked Pasenadi.

'Pardon me, Your Majesty, but in my reasoning it was Mahanama and his officers who were at fault, as it were their actions that led to this outcome,' the minister was very straightforward. 'The Sakyas ought to be taught a lesson.'

'You feel that we should attack Kapilavatthu and take Mahanama a prisoner?' questioned the king.

'I feel that it would be the correct thing to do.'

Hearing his minister, Pasenadi introspected for a while and then remarked, 'Kapilavatthu is Tathagata's homeland. I feel it would be unwise to attack it.'

***

The Sakya councillors travelled to Kusinagara to obtain Gautama's guidance on how to deal with the threat that loomed large on Kapilavatthu. However, they returned empty-handed.

'The Raja of Kapilavatthu has wronged, and he and his men should be prepared to face the consequences of their bad *kamma*,' The Awakened One passed his judgement to the councillors. He also did not give them a precise date of his arrival in Kapilavatthu.

Irrigators channel waters; fletchers straighten arrows; carpenters bend wood; the wise master themselves.

—Dhammapada

The gruelling life of a *dasa* is inconceivable for someone who has not witnessed their drudgery. Both the queen mother and the prince were victims of cruel fate. Though Vasabhakhatiya was not raised in royal luxury, the slog of a slave was definitely not meant for her tender body. As for Prince Vidudabha, who had grown up in sumptuousness, menial work was far beyond his competence.

Discussions, debates, and rumour-mongering over the enslavement of the future king of Kosala and the Rani Mai spread everywhere—in Kosala, its capital Savathi, as well as in other lands—like wildfire, as such an incident was never heard of before.

At night, when Vasabhakhatiya would lay on the hard bed, her dainty body would shriek in pain. Vidudabha, too, was unable to sleep contentedly on the stiff bed in the foul-smelling room, but he registered no protest. He toiled hard in silence under the sizzling sun, in the unremitting rain, and in the unbearable cold. He watched his mother fall victim to the lust of the rustic slaves while performing the arduous tasks without uttering a sound. She gradually turned into a feeble and a frail woman.

'You have become so weak, Mai,' Vidudabha softly said to her.

'You, too, have become so thin. I cannot even say that good times await you, my son,' Vasabhakhatiya ran her thin fingers through his hair. One of the supervisors came close to them and said, 'Your Highness, I know I am being cruel, but we have orders. I hope you understand ... '

'Yes, Supervisor, you are a kind man. But you need not worry. We will now depart,' Vidudabha and his mother took leave of each other. Vidudabha could sense that with every passing day, his hatred and anger were growing against his father Pasenadi and his grandfather Mahanama.

***

One night, worn out by the grinding labour of the day, Vidudabha had just shut his eyes when a soft knock on the door woke him up. Wondering who it might be, he opened the rickety door to find a turbaned man standing in the doorway. He had his face completely wrapped to conceal his identity. Looking at either side, the stranger pushed his way into the room. Once inside, the man dropped his covers. In the faint glow of a *dhibri* in the diminutive and decrepit room, Vidudabha found that the man was Digha Karayana, the senapati of Kosala.

'Jai Kosala! Salute to the Yuvraj of Kosala! I had to be very vigilant to come here. You never know, your movements might be tracked,' the senapati whispered and bowed to Vidudabha.

'Senapati, I am no more a prince; I'm just a slave. Please do not bow to me and do not honour me by coming to meet.'

'I understand your situation, Sire, but the truth is that you indeed are the Prince of Kosala and it cannot be denied.'

'What can I do for you, Senapati?' inquired Vidudabha softly.

'In the palace, in the city, and in the entire kingdom, everyone is unhappy to see their Rani Mai and Yuvraj labouring as slaves,' murmured Digha. 'It is indeed very difficult for us to see the inhuman labour which you and the Queen are subjected to. Wonder if the poor Queen can survive all this toil! The King has been so brutal towards the both of you. Even I have been the victim of his ruthless behaviour previously, Kumar.' Saying so, Digha narrated the tragic tale of Bandhula to Vidudabha.

'Oh, this is so lamentable, Senapati! You had never mentioned this distressing incident to me,' Vidudabha said, surprised at his father's hard-heartedness towards others.

'Kumar, keep patience. Very soon, you shall become the Maharaja of Kosala. I am only waiting for the opportune moment.'

'And how is that to come?'

'My army is with me, O Prince. We shall install you as the King of Kosala by ousting the present ruler, Maharaj Pasenadi,' muttered Digha, bringing his lips close to Vidudabha's ears. 'Kumar, till that moment, bear the torture that you have been subjected to, as this would toughen you up and prepare you to take charge of the kingdom of Kosala.'

The mind, when developed and cultivated, is soft and pliant.

—Mudu Sutta

The Buddha and Ananda, his closest disciple, arrived at Jethavan after a gap of a few years. Upon reaching there, he heard that Maharani Vasabhakhatiya and Yuvraj Vidudabha were still kept as slaves in the palace at Savathi. This deeply distressed The Enlightened One.

'*Bhantey*, we shall visit Maharaj Pasenadi right now and try to convince him to have his Rani and Yuvraj liberated from their afflictions. It's so saddening to hear about their condition,' the Buddha told Ananda.

***

'Maharaj, do you think that the judgment that you have conferred on two of your closest people is just? Do you not think that you have punished them for offences not perpetrated by them?' the Buddha questioned Pasenadi. The king did not answer. A pin-drop silence prevailed in the assembly as everyone eagerly waited for the king's reaction to Tathagata's question. But Pasenadi remained tight-lipped and lowered his head.

'I am, however, aware of the occurences that led you to pronounce such an abysmal verdict,' said the Buddha. Although he looked serene, his tone was obdurate.

'O, Master,' Pasenadi meekly protested and placed his view. 'Vasabhakhatiya was aware that she was not a princess but a *dasi*-

putri, yet she married me to become the Rani of Kosala. I found it to be a crime and, hence, as punishment, she has been sent among the *dasa*s, where she belongs. Vidudabha, being her son, cannot be taken as a prince either; therefore, he too was sent to the slave quarters.'

Buddha remained silent for a while and then softly said, 'True you are. But Maharaj, have you ever thought that she might be purely guiltless? That she might have been forced by Mahanama and his men against her own wishes to impersonate as the Princess of Kapilavatthu? Being a slave woman's daughter, perhaps, she could not oppose the arrangement.'

'No, I did not think of this, Honourable Tathagata.'

'Did you listen to her side of the story?'

'No, I did not.'

'As a king, should you not have heard her version as well?'

'Yes, O Blessed One.'

'It is sad that all you could think of was your own humiliation. Never once did you even try to understand the Queen's trauma. Dear Maharaj, what about your son, the young Rajkumar Vidudabha? What fault is his to be born as her son that you chastised him with such a harsh sentence?' The Buddha gazed straight into the eyes of Pasenadi and again asked, 'Does your blood not run in his veins too, O Maharaj Pasenadi?'

'Yes, Great Master,' Pasenadi replied feebly.

'As a king, you should always be on the side of truth and justice. Your erroneous decision of their punishment must have crushed both Maharani and Yuvraj for life. Your actions must have turned them against you. Maharaj, noble and good actions always result in good consequences, while bad *kamma*s bring equally bad outcomes. Therefore, to make amends of the ills that you have done, set them free immediately and give back to them the dignity of the Queen and the Prince of Kosala.'

Hearing this, a joyous commotion spread among the people in the court. Surprised, Pasenadi stared at the people in the assembly who were listening to the Buddha in exuberance, something that the king had not anticipated.

'As The Enlightened One has instructed, get Vasabhakhatiya and Vidudabha in the assembly,' Pasenadi ordered his minister rather grudgingly. The minister and a few nobles hastened towards the slave quarters to fetch the rani and the rajkumar.

'Master, if Mahanama and the Sakyas are responsible for such an insult to Kosala, should they go unpunished? Should we not declare war upon them?' asked Pasenadi irritably.

'War is no solution for the wrongs done by people,' Tathagata said, with his eyes half closed. 'Just think of the numerous innocent people who may be killed in the war only because you seek to avenge the slur on you.'

***

An uproar of cries rang through the court when the queen and the prince were brought in. No one could recognize them in their soiled clothes covering their mucky and feeble bodies. Deep sighs of lament echoed in the large hall. Pasenadi was astonished at the reaction of his people. Both Vasabhakhatiya and Vidudabha touched the feet of the Buddha with great reverence and then greeted the people in the hall. The assembly resonated with cries, 'Jai Maharani Vasabhakhatiya, Jai Yuvraj Vidudabha, Jai Kosala!'

Maharaja Pasenadi ordered Vasabhakhatiya to stand before him.

'Vasabhakhatiya, I desired to marry a Sakya princess. Your father did not wish to send his own daughter to marry me, as I have been informed that Mahanama and the Sakyas would never let their princess marry a Kosala. Is it true?'

Vasabhakhatiya nodded.

'I was even informed that your father Mahanama and his councillors schemed to send you, a *dasi-putri*, to marry me, impersonating you as a Sakya princess. Is that correct?'

Vasabhakhatiya nodded again.

'Did you give your consent to this?' the king unswervingly questioned Vasabhakhatiya. The queen remained silent.

'Answer me!'

Vasabhakhatiya still did not voice a reply.

'You knew about the conspiracy and yet you agreed to be a part of this deceit. Why did you not resist?' asked the king. The queen did not utter a word.

Vidudabha stood watching the entire episode silently. A strong anger was fermenting inside him against his father.

'You made her slog as a slave for so many years and now you ask this? Is this your justice, Maharaj Pasenadi?' Vidudabha lashed out, unable to control himself anymore. Pasenadi, who was not prepared for his son's flare, looked at him for a while and then raised his hands to silence him.

'Answer me, Vasabhakhatiya,' commanded the king.

'The daughter of a *dasi*, I was forced into this marriage. How can people like us object to injustices and excesses done to us?' Vasabhakhatiya confessed to Maharaja Pasenadi about the pains and sufferings she had endured. Perhaps, this was her last too.

Pasenadi looked at his wife for a moment. 'As instructed by our venerable Great Master, the Buddha, I am setting you both, Vasabhakhatiya and Vidudabha, free from slavery and reinstating you as the Rani and the Rajkumar of Kosala,' Pasenadi declared disdainfully.

Vasabhakhatiya bowed at her husband king with deep respect, while young Vidudabha turned and walked away without even looking at his father. Pasenadi felt humiliated by his son's attitude in front of his subjects and court officials, but said nothing. Tathagata observed the happenings and closed his eyes as his heart ached on sensing the future course of events.

***

Later in the day, after returning to Jethavan, Buddha prophesized to Ananda, 'I sense a storm approaching and I must try to prevent it from evolving into a perilous tempest, else hundreds of thousands shall die. But the question is, can it be done?'

Through diligence, vigilance, self-restraint and subjugation of the senses, the wise aspirant makes an island for himself that no flood could engulf.

—Dhammapada

That the powerful army of Kosala may invade Kapilavatthu any day and take hold of Mahanama was a fear rife in Kapilavatthu. An emergency meeting was called at the *santhagara* by the council.

'Since we cannot defend ourselves from the powerful Kosala army, we need to seek help from the *ganarajya*s of Vajji, Lichhavi, Malla, and Koliya,' declared Mahanama.

'I agree to this,' responded Harita.

'We should talk to our fellow *ganarajya*s soon, for we could be invaded any moment now,' Anantha, another councillor, added.

'The fact that Gautama is a Sakya and that Pasenadi and Maharani Mallika are followers of Tathagata's *dhamma* have perhaps stalled the invasion. But we do not know what awaits tomorrow or how long Pasenadi would remain inert. We have to send messages for military assistance to our neighbouring *ganarajya*s,' said Mahanama.

***

The tortures and humiliation on the prince and his mother by both his grandfather and father snatched away the innocence and purity of the naive Vidudabha. After his redemption from slavery, he barely talked to anyone other than his mother and Digha. His features hardened and a graveness gradually set in, replacing the jollity on his countenance. Whosoever saw this gradual transformation in his personality presumed that a profound rage was brewing within him that was to erupt any day. Nobody knew when, how, and on whom. Only Vasabhakhatiya and Digha understood the agony that was gnawing at the prince within. Vengeance, it seemed, could only douse the fire of disgrace and humiliation that incessantly smouldered inside him.

Vidudabha loved no one other than his mother Vasabhakhatiya. Whatever empathy and compassion that was left in him was meant for her. He knew that his mother's heart was devoid of even the smallest happiness, as Mahanama and Pasenadi had converted her life into a living hell; a life which she accepted in silence without any opposition. Vasabhakhatiya's unremitting trauma and poor food intake during her enslavement resulted in the deterioration of her health. Soon, she took to bed. The queen began sinking. Her husband Pasenadi never did come once to see his ailing wife. The medicines of the royal *vaidyas* and the *kavirajas* seemed ineffective. They observed that the queen did not seem to have a desire to live. Vidudabha silently watched the proceedings. Sitting by his mother's bed, the yuvraj would run his fingers through his mother's hair and over her feeble and aching body.

'Forgive me, my boy. I could offer you no happiness as a mother,' the bedridden queen would weakly open her eyes and say with tears rolling down from them.

Rajkumar Vidudabha was not sent to Takshashila, as was promised by his father earlier. On the contrary, the resident Brahmin teachers continued to teach him, while Senapati Digha educated him about the intricacies of war and weapons.

Maharaja Pasenadi had never forgiven either his queen or the prince. No sooner the thought that the blood of a low-born slave ran inside his queen and the prince came to his mind than he was filled with revulsion and ire for them. He would maltreat Vidudabha in front of everyone even at his smallest gaffe. The prince would silently endure his father's slanders. His eyes would turn moist when he remembered his father's affectionate touches and sweet chatter in his younger days.

***

Pasenadi was aging and he knew that he had to declare Vidudabha as his rightful heir, despite his sternest detestation of the idea.

'Why this worry, Maharaj?' his minister would put in. 'We have Yuvraj Vidudabha as our next king.'

'I dare not make Vidudabha my successor. Do you not know that in him runs the blood of a *dasi-putri*?' asked Pasenadi.

A silence descended in the court as no one could think of a possible way out of this dilemma. Pasenadi called for the *rajjyotishi*.

'Is a marriage possible for me at this age, *rajjyotishi*? You see, Kosala needs an heir. Can you examine my horoscope in detail and see if there is a possible alteration in my destiny?' Pasenadi asked the chief astrologer.

The *rajjyotishi* spread the king's horoscope on the floor. Assisted by two of his aides, he began studying the birth chart contemplatively.

'Maharaj,' said the *rajjyotishi* after a long time. 'After studying your horoscope comprehensively, we found that your future neither holds any marriage nor another son. Honourable Prince Vidudabha is indeed the future King of Kosala.'

Look upon the world as a bubble, look upon it as a mirage.

—Dhammapada

One morning, two of Vidudabha's cousins pestered him to ride to the marketplace. Though the prince refused at first, the cousins did not give up; finally, Vidudabha had to concede to their insistence and the trio rode into town. They reached one of the busiest marketplaces in the capital, where the street was buzzing with people. Seeing the prince, the citizens saluted Vidudabha and moved aside to make way for him and his cousins. An old beggar woman, however, impeded their path. Being disabled, she was unable to cross the street quickly. This enraged the prince's cousins.

'Come on, old hag! Move aside, fast,' one of the cousins scorned. She found it difficult to drag herself hurriedly, no matter how hard she tried. Alighting from his horse, Vidudabha slowly walked towards the old woman.

'Come Mai, hold my hand.' He pulled her up on his lap, walked slowly across the road, and gently placed her at the sidewalk. The old woman blessed the prince with tear-soaked eyes. Vidudabha looked at the beggar woman for a moment, then took out his diamond-studded gold ring from his right-hand middle finger and put it in her begging bowl.

'Mai, sell this to the *sonar* and you shall not need to beg the rest of your life. But be very cautious while selling it. You could be swindled.' Vidudabha returned to his horse and ordered one of his guards, 'Somra, stay here and help the woman sell the ring. See that no one tricks her and that she gets the right amount from the *sonar* without any hassle. Then drop her home.'

Vidudabha was familiar with the names of most of the soldiers and the workforce of the palace. By this time, a crowd had congregated around him. The people, witness to the entire episode, were indeed amazed to find their prince so compassionate. Soon, the people sang his praises loudly, 'Jai Yuvraj Vidudabha! Jai!' Vidudabha raised his arms in a gesture to stop the cheer and rode away with his cousins.

The incident, however, did not end here. In the evening, Vidudabha rode into the barracks of the soldiers in search of Somra. Seeing the rajkumar, a hubbub spread among the soldiers.

'I am looking for Somra,' Vidudabha told one of the sentries.

'Yes, Honourable Prince,' he replied.

In a moment, Somra appeared before him.

'Somra, how did things go with the old woman?'

'Yuvraj, the *sonar* did try to trick the woman, but when he heard that the ring was the prince's gift, he paid her a hefty amount,' replied Somra.

'Good. Did you drop the old woman at her house?'

'Yes, Sir, I did,' Somra assured Vidudabha, and he walked away contentedly.

Although Prince Vidudabha was widely known for his egotism, numerous stories of his selflessness and benevolence for the impoverished and deprived were popular in the city. Little did Vidudabha himself and his well-wishers know that this compassion was soon to become a thing of the past.

***

The strained relationship between the father and the son persisted, and they never conversed with one another unless there was a pressing matter. Although the maharaja had lessened his tirades at Vidudabha, the prince was kept aloof from all state ceremonies by not being invited. Vidudabha never questioned his father for such affronts; he silently bore the humiliation. Vasabhakhatiya, his mother, never really recuperated from her illness, which transpired from the continuous tribulations that life had conferred on her.

Months passed, but Pasenadi still did not visit his ailing queen for he was unable to forget the deceit of his wife and her father. It was only Vidudabha who, perceiving her intense affliction, sat by her bed and looked after her conscientiously. Deep inside, he fostered extreme hatred towards his father and grandfather as he knew that both were responsible for his mother's condition.

Digha, like a true friend, stood by Vidudabha's side. He could feel the prince's wrath silently building inside him against Pasenadi, Mahanama, and the Sakyas.

'Have patience, Kumar. Soon, you shall become the King of Kosala,' Digha would placate him.

'Yes, Senapati,' Vidudabha would say quietly with grit in his intense gaze.

***

That evening, Vidudabha was very restless. He hadn't experienced such restiveness earlier. Was this a premonition of something dreadful about to happen? An image of his ailing mother flashed before his eyes and he darted out of his room.

Entering his mother's chamber, Vidudabha found a few female attendants and *vaidyas* stooping low on the queen. Seeing the yuvraj enter, the women stepped aside but the *vaidyas* continued to examine her pulses. His mother seemed to be in some deep pain as she tossed and turned on her bed uneasily. Sitting at her bedside, he ran his fingers softly through the thinning hair of his sick mother. Her eyes had sunk deep and her cheeks were hollow.

Feeling the comforting touch of her son, tears flowed from her closed eyes. Vasabhakhatiya placed her skinny hands on her son's. With a lot of effort, she opened her eyes.

'My boy,' her voice was a little more than a murmur. 'All your life, you have received no love but abhorrence. Your grandfather has no love for you. Your father, who once loved you so dearly, hates you now because of me. I have no news of your grandmother who loved you so dearly. Even I could not look after you well, like a mother should.' Vasabhakhatiya seemed out of breath. After a while, she again slowly opened her tired eyes to gaze at her loving son.

Vidudabha's right hand was already holding hers. She tried to press it, but could not. Collecting her breath, she resumed talking with great difficulty, 'I ... am leaving ... you forever ... a ... lone ... in this cru ... el wo ... rld. If pos ... sible, for ... give me, my chi ... ld ... , forgive ... me ... ,' a muffled moan escaped her throat and then she fell silent.

Forever.

Vidudabha understood that his mother was eventually liberated from all her agony.

Forever.

He kept looking at her for long. His face stiffened. After a while, tears gushed out of his eyes, but no sound escaped him. One of the *vaidyas* stepped forward and, swaying his palms over the dead queen's face, shut her gaping mouth and closed her gawking eyes. Although Pasenadi had not bothered to visit Vasabhakhatiya's room for several months, the news of her demise shook him badly. She was cremated on the banks of the sacred Achiravati River. The news of Maharani Vasabhakhatiya's death was conveyed to Kapilavatthu.

***

Maharani Vasabhakhatiya's *shradhya* rites were performed by her son, Yuvraj Vidudabha, on the twelfth day. The prince kept his father from performing any ritual for his dead wife. He, however, did not obstruct Pasenadi from attending the rites; neither did he stop his father from offering a brick in the construction of a *thuppa* on her mortal remains.

The construction of Vasabhakhatiya's *thuppa*, dutifully administered by Vidudabha, took about ten days to be completed. After it was done, Vidudabha talked to his dead mother, sitting beside her memorial and tenderly caressing it. He felt that it would be unfair to forgive the sins of his grandfather and father who were both responsible for his mother's tormenting life that eventually led to her death.

***

Once the rituals were over, Pasenadi sent word to his son Vidudabha that he wished to meet him. The prince instantly declined his appeal, stating that he had no desire to meet him. This denial from his son came as a blow to the king. Maharani Mallika could comprehend that all the foregoing events had strained the father–son relationship.

'Maharaj, I do understand that your anxiety comes from the loss of Rani Vasabhakhatiya and also from Rajkumar Vidudabha's disrespect towards you. I suggest that you visit Tathagata, as his sermons will help you heal your wounds,' she suggested.

'You are right, Maharani. How well you understand me even after so many years. I shall surely visit him. Wonder where he is now,' said the king.

'I have been told that the Buddha has encamped near Veshali.'

'Good. I shall visit the Buddha at the soonest.'

'Since it is summer, I would suggest that you travel in the cool of the night, in which case you would reach Veshali by morning.'

'That indeed is a good idea. Let me decide the date of my journey,' Pasenadi smiled at Mallika.

Having entered upon the path (of dhamma) you will come to an end of your suffering.

—Dhammapada

Ascetics in ancient India would drift from one spot to the other, refraining from staying at one place for long, lest an attachment develops for it and its people. They knew that such attachments lead to sorrow. Being true to this principle of non-attachment, Buddha and Ananda too wandered. In the course of their wayfaring, Buddha and Ananda put up at an open space of a sparingly wooded jungle off the highway to Rajagaha in the outskirts of Veshali. This was the space where the *bhikkhus* had once stayed during one of their earlier visits.

Morning.

Pasenadi, escorted by a few of his guards, rode night-long and eventually arrived at the fringes of Veshali the following morning. Rummaging around for a long time, they finally stumbled upon the site where the Buddha and Ananda had camped. The *bhikkhus* were deep in meditation in the cool shade of a large banyan tree.

It was the month of Jyeshtha, and the blazing sun breathed fire. Tired of the night-long voyage, the soldiers prepared a resting place for Pasenadi in the cool shade of a thick mango tree, where the king decided to relax till the Buddha rose from his dhyana. The sentries brought him water from the river flowing nearby, which he drank to his heart's fulfilment. As always, Maharaja Pasenadi had come to the Buddha as a common man, leaving behind all the major insignias that distinguished him as the king.

By doing so, Pasenadi attempted to practice detachment from the vanity and pride of being a king, while submitting himself to the Buddha's *dhamma*.

Soon, the old and the weary king dozed off in the cool shade of the mango tree. Pasenadi did not know for how long he had slept when voices woke him up. He sat up with a start to find the Buddha conversing with a few villagers.

'So you have woken up, Maharaj. Come, Sire, join us. You should have done the morning *vipassana* with us.' Pasenadi walked up to the Buddha, kissed his feet, and sat with the villagers.

'Come, sit by me, O King.'

'No, Master, I am blessed by sitting at your feet and listening you speak,' replied Pasenadi. The Buddha continued his conversation with the villagers, 'Yes, Brother, please go on with what you were about to tell me.'

'Master, the Brahmins always look down upon us as outcastes. They hate us and even avoid our shadows,' a villager said.

'Do not worry, for the Brahmins do not know who an outcaste is. Brother, an outcaste is one who is resentful, indignant, evil, cruel, and dishonest, and has flawed opinions of people and things. He is an outcaste who harms living beings and has no sympathy for them, whosoever they may be, once born or twice (*dwija*). My brother, you are not an outcaste. If one goes to a house where he is offered pure food but doesn't honour the host, that person is an outcaste. Be it a Brahmin, a meditative person, or a beggar, if he swindles and lies, the person is indeed an outcaste.

'My friend, a person even born in a Brahmin family is not a Brahmin. One's actions and knowledge, and not his birth, would make him a Brahmin. Similarly, a person born in a mlechha household cannot be held as an outcaste. His actions would make him an outcaste, and not his birth.

'Just as the great rivers Achiravati, Ganga, Yamuna, and Mahi lose their names and identities on reaching the sea and become one with the ocean, similarly the one who renounces the world and joins the *sangha* of the *dhamma* loses his previous name and identity and disassociates from one's *vanna*. Finally, I pray that *karuna* and *daya* fill up the hearts of everyone, that everyone sheds their anger, and that no one hates another. Radiate your kindness to the entire world,' Tathagata paused speaking thus. 'That shall be all for today,' the Buddha concluded, and the villagers bowed to him and departed.

Turning towards Pasenadi, he inquired, 'What brings you here, O Mighty King? I can understand that you have travelled the entire night to reach here. The matter must be urgent then.'

'O Master, Rani Vasabhakhatiya has passed away. My son does not obey me even when I summon him. He has the least regard for me. Whom shall I crown as the next king of Kosala after me? I am so worried, O Holy One.'

'Your qualms are indeed valid, Maharaj Pasenadi. But then, your son's behaviour towards you is the result of your misdeeds. Can you not see that?'

'I know, O Blessed One. That's why I am here to seek solace from the tribulations of the world.'

'It is good, Maharaj, that you have finally learnt that the world is a place of apprehension, sorrow, decay, and death. We may be here for some more days before we leave for Rajagaha. Stay with us. Enjoy the open skies. Join us all in the *pindapata* and practice *vipassana* with us. You would soon be a reformed person with abundant happiness.'

If you do good work you will reap good results and bad works will have bad results as a good seed if carefully planted will give us good fruit.

—Dhammapada

Savathi.

It was still dark when Digha Karayana was informed about Maharaja Pasenadi's sudden retreat to Veshali in the night. He was further conveyed that the maharaja would not be back for a few days. Digha was aware that during such spiritual trips to the Buddha, Pasenadi was in the habit of leaving behind his regal insignias in the palace. Digha sat up in his bed and pondered. Was this the opportunity he had been waiting for all these years to establish Vidudabha as the king of Kosla and, in the process, avenge the death of Bandhula and his family? Perhaps, yes. He suddenly became alert. He should get his plans in order as soon as possible.

On that hot and sultry afternoon, the residents of the palace were catnapping inside closed doors. A few men and women proceeded stealthily towards the dark alleys of the palace for an appointment with Digha. No one usually accessed these dark passageways, so it was reasonably safe to hold a furtive meeting here. Digha was already waiting there anxiously for his followers to turn up. The people, tired of the prejudices and the injustices of the king, had pledged their allegiance to Digha.

Many a time, the group had met earlier at different secretive venues to discuss their plan of overthrowing Maharaja Pasenadi.

That afternoon, too, they decided to meet in a secluded area inside the palace at Senapati Digha's beckoning. Without much ado, he proclaimed that the moment of change for the betterment of Savathi and Kosala, about which they had been dreaming for long, has finally arrived. Pasenadi had to be removed and Prince Vidudabha installed as the new king. Digha, along with the conspirators, meticulously chalked out the plan by which the coup d'état was to be staged that very night in Maharaja Pasenadi's absence.

Night.

Like cats on prowl, Digha and a few of his trusted men moved swiftly yet noiselessly towards the heavily guarded king's room. In a moment, lifeless bodies of the guards lay dead on the floor with their throats slit opened. Then they knocked softly on the door of the king's chamber where Maharani Mallika was sleeping, unaware of the happenings outside.

The door was opened by one of the female guards of the queen, who let Digha and his men enter the royal chamber. The female guards went to the sleeping maharani and softly called her.

'Honourable Queen, wake up.'

Mallika woke up with a start and was struck with sudden fear to find Digha and his soldiers standing by her bed.

'What's the meaning of all this? What is going on, Senapati?' the queen shuddered, yet demanded with confidence.

'Maharani, we do not mean to harm you. We are here to take possession of the emblems of Maharaj Pasenadi—his shoes, turban, and his sword,' replied Digha with a firmness in his voice.

'Why? They are no business of yours, Senapati,' Mallika replied harshly.

'Indeed they are, Respectable Queen. We are deposing Maharaj Pasenadi and crowning Vidudabha as the succeeding king of Kosala at this very moment. So we need these insignias for the new king's enthronement.'

'This is treason! Guards, guards! Arrest these men,' ordered the queen.

'No one will come at your call, Maharani. All the guardsmen and women in the palace are ours now, and so is the army. We all want to do away with the reign of Maharaj Pasenadi and install Vidudabha as our new king. And now, if you could hurry up and furnish us with the imperial seals....' Queen Mallika nervously pointed her shaky finger towards a large chest. One of the guards raised its lid and fished out the royal turban, a pair of shoes, and the sword from it.

'Thank you, Honourable Queen,' Digha said while leaving.

'Before you leave, Senapati, may I ask you what was the necessity for all this when Vidudabha would have become the king of Kosala by natural choice after Maharaj Pasenadi?'

'Maharani, we know that. But we are doing this out of our love for Yuvraj Vidudabha. If he became the king by natural choice, could we have punished Maharaj Pasenadi for all the ordeals he had put Rani Vasabhakhatiya, Yuvraj Vidudabha, my uncle Bandhula, his children and wife, and even the numerous people of Kosala through?' Senapati Digha's face stiffened. 'He has to suffer for all his sins....'

'Will you kill him?' Maharani Mallika asked Digha fearfully.

'That, Maharani, will depend on the course of events,' saying this, Digha and his people walked out in haste, locking the queen behind.

***

Oblivious to the occurrences in the palace, Vidudabha was sleeping contentedly when he heard sharp knocks on his door. Waking up with a flinch, he called out, 'Who is it?'

'Kumar, it is your Senapati,' came a muffled reply from the other side of the door. Vidudabha hurriedly opened it to find Digha and the troop standing in the entrance.

'What is all this, Senapati? At this time of the night?' asked Vidudabha surprisingly.

'Did I not promise you, Kumar, that I shall help you in becoming the King of Kosala? The time is finally here.' Digha then elucidated him briefly about the string of events that occured that day. He added, 'Kumar, please make your way to the assembly now. Everyone, including the nobles, the ministers, the advisors, and the *rajpurohit*, would be there.'

'What for, Senapati?'

'My dear Yuvraj, there, in the grand assembly, you shall be crowned the Maharaja of Kosala.'

Do not become attached to what is pleasing, nor to what is displeasing.

—Dhammapada

Conflict broke out between the forces loyal to Maharaja Pasenadi and those to Senapati Digha and Prince Vidudabha when news broke that the maharaja's stately symbols have been appropriated by Senapati Digha to ordain Yuvraj Vidudabha as the next king by overthrowing his father Pasenadi.

Meanwhile, in the palace that night, Vidudabha was escorted to the royal assembly by a group of soldiers and a retinue of nobles. The prime minister, deputy ministers, nobles, advisors, the *rajpurohit*, other officials, and a large number of prominent people of Savathi gathered in the night at the behest of the senapati of Kosala, who, standing beside the royal seat, awaited the arrival of the future king.

Vidudabha walked into the assembly with much grace and aplomb. A great clamour rose in the hall the moment everyone caught a glimpse of the prince. Digha gestured Vidudabha to stand by his side.

'Prime minister, ministers, advisors, nobles, *rajpurohit* and other Brahmins, respectable citizens, soldiers, and guards,' addressed Digha in the court. 'Being a warrior, I cannot make a suitable speech. But I can say that with the blessings of Tathagata, we, the citizens of the *mahajanapada* of Kosala, have decided tonight to declare Yuvraj Vidudabha as the Maharaja of Kosala.'

The *rajpurohit*, along with a few other Brahmins, was summoned for the coronation of Vidudabha.

'*Rajpurohit*, the *homa* and the other rites can be conducted later in the day. The crowning needs to be done at the earliest,' Digha whispered a stern instruction into the ears of the royal priest. In a few moments, the Brahmins commenced with their chanting of Vedic mantras. Vidudabha, Digha, and other dignitaries of the kingdom took their respective seats. The *rajpurohit* and Vidudabha then sat on the floor and began the rituals.

'Senapati, put the royal shoes before the prince,' the *rajpurohit* told Digha after completing the rituals shortly. The pair of royal footwear was brought by two women on a large golden salver. Digha offered them to Vidudabha, requesting him to put them on.

'Now place the royal turban on his head,' said the *rajpurohit*. Digha held the imperial turban securely with both his hands and set it on Vidudabha's head. Following this, the prince was graced with the royal red *phonta*, a mix of vermilion, sandal paste, and the sacred mustard oil on his forehead. Thereafter, the *rajpurohit* pasted a few rice grains on the tilak and sprinkled a few more on Vidudabha's head while murmuring an indistinct mantra. The *rajpurohit* then graced Vidudabha with *aarti*, the holy light, while chanting the Vedic mantras and blowing the conch. Vidudabha slowly rose from his seat and respectfully touched the *rajpurohit*'s feet while he blessed him.

'Your Highness,' proclaimed the *rajpurohit*. 'You are now declared the Maharaja of Kosala. O Maharaj, the throne is all yours.' The priest asked Vidudabha to take his place on the regal seat. The royal assembly resonated with loud calls, 'Jai Maharaj Vidudabha, Jai Kosala' from all directions, with conch shells resounding across the huge room. Slowly, Vidudabha seated himself on the throne of Kosala.

'Senapati Digha Karayana, you may now adorn the king with the royal sword,' said the *rajpurohit*. Digha subsequently presented Maharaja Vidudabha with the imperial sword of his dynasty, while everyone in the court kept cheering for the newly anointed king.

***

'Citizens of Savathi and Kosala,' Maharaja Vidudabha's imposing voice reverberated in the assembly, 'I have been crowned the king of this great *mahajanapada* of Kosala. Like my predecessors, I, as the father of this great kingdom, pledge to take care of all the citizens. I will revere the brahmins, the *acela*s, the digamvaras, the svetambaras, the *bhikkhus*, and all other holy men. I shall work for the farmers and build more irrigation canals for them. I assure to work for the welfare of the artisans and the tradesmen, see that taxes do not become a burden for the poor, and make the highway free of brigands. I further vow to work for the benefit of the forests, birds, ponds, animals, and hills. I also bow reverentially at the lotus feet of the Buddha.' Saying this, Vidudabha, the new king of Kosala, stood up, holding his royal sword high up in the air, and let out a call, 'Jai Kosala!'

'Jai Kosala, Jai Maharaj Vidudabha!' everyone hailed.

At death a person abandons what he construes as mine.

—Dhammapada

Digha dispatched an envoy to Maharaja Ajatsattu at Rajagaha with a message that Vidudabha has been pronounced the king of Kosala. The note which the messenger carried comprised not only the detailed information of the anointing of Vidudabha, but also about Pasenadi's journey to the Buddha at Veshali. The missive even included a reminder that since Ajatsattu, the Magadha *naresh*, was fond of his brother-in-law Vidudabha, Kosala expected full support from him.

The slaughtering of those loyal to Pasenadi and of those opposed to the crowning of Vidudabha continued till the following day. Mutilated dead bodies lay scattered all across the city. By afternoon, all dissent was silenced.

'No news of Vidudabha's enthronement should leave the city walls unless instructed by the King,' ordered Senapati Digha. By evening, an unsettling calmness prevailed in Savathi.

Digha, in the meantime, had already ordered the closure of all the gates of Savathi so that even the slightest hearsay of the incidents could not be leaked out by someone inside the city or by anyone entering it. In spite of all the preventive measures by Digha, reports of the rebellion reached Pasenadi late in the afternoon. Pasenadi, who was incalculably content on being enlightened by the Buddha's sermons about the Middle Path, received a severe jolt on learning of the occurrences at Savathi. But that Maharani Mallika was safe comforted him a little. Pasenadi discovered that his sentries had fled, and he was left alone to defend himself. He approached the Buddha in the hope to seek his advice on his future agenda of actions. The Venerated One was in profound dhyana. To wake him up for his sake, Pasenadi felt, would be imprudent.

He thought it sensible not to return to Savathi, as all his trustworthy people may either have been massacred or imprisoned. His misgiving was about Mallika though. She was safe now, but would they kill her afterwards? The wisest thing, he conjectured, was to trek all the way to his daughter and son-in-law Ajatsattu in Rajagaha and, maybe later, with the assistance of the Magadha army, attack Vidudabha.

With no money to buy himself food for the night and neither a sword to defend himself from robbers in the highway and animals in the dense forests, Pasenadi embarked on his journey to Rajagaha. Trudging along in the coolness of the star-spangled night and in the merciless heat of the scorching sun the following day, he reached Rajagaha. But the news that Pasenadi was heading towards Rajagaha had already reached the maharaja of Magadha. By the time old Pasenadi reached Rajagaha in the oppressive heat, he was exhausted, thirsty, and starving. He somehow dragged his exasperated self to the fort of Ajatsattu to find the gates slowly close down on him. He kept banging at the large entry gates of the walled city, but to no avail; they remained shut.

Ultimately, owing to extreme fatigue and dehydration in the blistering heat, Pasenadi collapsed on the ground and died.

***

Reports of the death of Pasenadi reached Savathi, but no one dare mourned his demise. Neither did any one have the audacity to speak up against the manner Vidudabha was crowned the king. The news of her husband's death was communicated to Maharani Mallika. Shocked by the heart-rending news, she broke into loud wails and fainted. The palace *vaidyas* and the womenfolk attended to her. News reached Maharaja Vidudabha that the remains of the former king would arrive the next morning.

A wooden sarcophagus containing the dead body of Pasenadi arrived from Rajagaha the following noon. The queen, accompanied by her women relations, fell on her dead husband and cried in loud rhythmic moans, as bucolic women still do in villages. She cursed and wailed loudly, crying out that had she not advised her husband to go to the Buddha, this catastrophe would not have transpired.

Pasenadi was cremated on the banks of the Achiravati River, and his ashes were subsequently buried with full state honour. A *thuppa* was decided to be erected on the remains of the dead king, adjacent to the *thuppa* of the dead Queen Vasabhakhatiya, after his *shradhya* ceremony.

Pasenadi's *shradhya* was conducted by his wife Maharani Mallika on the twelfth day of his cremation. During its observance, Vidudabha did not desert the venue even for a bare moment. After the ceremony, he, along with his half-sister Vajira, escorted Maharani Mallika to her room and helped her get some rest. Before leaving the room, the new king advised the attending *vaidyas* and the women attendants to nurse her with utmost care, for he had lost his own mother and could not, by any chance, afford to lose his *badi* mai.

***

Late in the dusk, Maharaja Vidudabha was seen riding with a few of his sentries to the *thuppa* of his mother Vasabhakhatiya. Alighting from his horse, Vidudabha slowly went towards the mound while his armed men waited. He hugged the *thuppa* with his open arms and kissed the monument beneath which the bones of his mother lay. His tears drenched the earth.

'Mai,' he murmured sniffing. 'The one who agonized and dishonoured you all your life is now dead, and I am the king. You did not live to see this. Bless me so that I can now seek vengeance from Mahanama and the Sakyas who ruined our lives. Give me strength, O Mother, so that I can keep my promise and bring solace to your grievous heart ... '

Whatever precious jewel there is in the heavenly worlds,
there is nothing comparable to one who is awakened.

—Sutta Nipata

Afternoon.

The Buddha roamed the streets of a village when a middle-aged person blocked their path.

'You are the Buddha?' enquired the man angrily.

'So they say,' Tathagata replied calmly.

'I have heard your sermons. Do you think I can really overcome my sorrows and sufferings by following your path?' asked the wrathful man. Siddhartha realized that the person was filled with so much hatred and anger that he would never understand his response. So he chose to remain silent.

'Why don't you reply, you old preacher?' The man's vexation and irritation was clearly perceptible on his features. A small flock of villagers were drawn towards the squabble. Seeing Tathagata, the villagers bowed to him and many even touched his feet. The veneration of the villagers towards the Buddha enraged the person even more.

'You fools, why do you adore him? Can you not see that he is a fraud, a fake?' The man's abuses continued, but the Buddha did not react. The villagers grabbed the man and tried to push him away.

'Go away! You always malign everyone. Today, you did not spare even our great Tathagata!' The Buddha smiled and stopped the villagers.

'My brother, you are in great pain and suffering and that is what you are offering to the world. I have received some mangoes in my course of *pindapata*. They indeed are very sweet. Here, take them, my brother. The sweetness of the fruits will sweeten the bitterness within you.' Tathagata extended a few mangoes to the infuriated man.

'Why should I take anything from someone like you? I refuse to accept your mangoes.'

'Alright, Brother. If your refuse to accept my offerings, then whose would they become?'

'They will be yours, old monk,' replied the angry man with vanity.

'Similarly, Brother, if I refuse to accept your slander and abuse, whose insult would it become?' asked the Buddha with a soft smile on his lips. This made the man all the more furious; but then, suddenly, he fell silent. Perhaps he understood what The Enlightened One was trying to explicate. The Buddha moved on before the man could speak any further.

***

The sun had already set, yet the fading vestige of the dusk remained. The birds had returned to their nests and were screeching loudly in the trees of Venuvan. The villagers who congregated to hear the sermons of their beloved Buddha had now left. As darkness was setting in, Moggallana brought in an earthen lamp and placed it under a peepul tree, adjacent to where the Blessed One sat meditatively in the lotus posture. He placed two stones on either side of the lamp to protect the flame from the blowing wind. The disciples slowly assembled around the Buddha.

'*Bhantey*, let me tell you once again that the world is a large platter of *dukkha*,' the Buddha began with his lotus eyes closed. 'You saw how Pasenadi died in sorrow and his death brought *dukkha* to his queen and his loved ones. His misery was the consequence of his wrong actions. Had he not treated his wife and his son so wrongfully, this suffering could have been averted,' the Buddha paused for a while. He again continued, 'We keep taking birth on this earth due to our unfulfilled desires and to suffer the consequences of the *kamma*s of our previous births.

'The mind causes all the problems. We need to learn to bring it in our control, or rather have it disciplined. Else, the undisciplined mind will create much disorder, annoyance, and harm in our lives. A disciplined mind, free from attachments, will make one liberated from worries and be happy. The control of the mind comes from dhyana and from surrendering to *dhamma*. You may read many holy books or hear or even speak holy words, but these will be of no good unless you act upon them. Practice dhyana regularly, lest it becomes too late.

'*Bhantey*, like many times earlier, I repeat that the *maijhima patipada* or the Middle Path of both the extreme life approaches helps in developing spiritual knowledge and assists in accepting life as it is. I know that you all are living the Middle Path as I have instructed, yet I keep telling you about this *maijhima patipada*. Avoid the extreme paths in life. The Middle Path is like the strings of the veena where, if you tighten up the strings too much, they may snap. On the other hand, neither can you play with too loose or wobbly strings. These two strings in their extreme positions can produce no music. For the best use of the strings, therefore, it is desirable to keep them in the middle position from which sweet music would flow,' the Buddha ended. Speaking at a stretch, due to old age, The Enlightened One became exhausted. After meditating for some time, he resumed.

'Similar to the strings' position in the veena, several people and sects too adopt harsh methods in their spiritual lives as self-mortification to attain *nibbana*. Remember that since this is an extreme path that leads to pain, one can never attain *nibbana* through it. The other extreme of life is actually assumed by the common man, who lives in corporeal pleasures that are attachments to materialism and will lead to *dukkha*. Hence, this life too is of another extreme. Accepting life in the middle path between the two extreme paths is required. The Middle Path subdues excitement and brings inner peace and happiness. The outer world, therefore, cannot assert any influence on you and you will be a happy person. I think that should be all for today. I shall speak again tomorrow after our morning *vipassana*.' The *bhikkhus* turned in for the night after their meal and dhyana.

The following morning, after their dhyana, the *sangha* gathered around Tathagata.

'What a splendid morning, *Bhantey*,' The Venerated One recommenced his sermons. 'Today, let's talk about the Four Noble Truths. Although you all have heard me speak of this several times, and you do practice them, yet I repeat them time and again. Taking cue from the incidents in Kosala, the first truth we learn is that the world is a place of *dukkha*. The second truth, which you all know, is *samudaya* or the cause of this *dukkha* or suffering that comes from attachments. The third truth is *nirodha* or its cessation, also known as *nibbana*. The fourth truth is the Eightfold Path or the *ariyo atthangiko maggo*—right views, right conduct, right living, right speech, right effort, right consciousness, right meditation, and right intention—that helps one end the painful cycle of rebirth and liberates the person from *samsara* by attaining *nibbana*. You all must already know these, yet I entreat you not to forget them ever,' Tathagata narrated his *vyakhana* very gently by closing his eyes and by raising his right hand.

'*Bhantey*, I remind you again to indulge in *vipassana* to bring *metta*, *karuna*, *mudita*, and *upekkha* into your lives. Your *karuna* or compassion and *metta* or kindness should be for all, be it humans or other life forms. Happiness of all should bring *mudita* or joy to you. Be grateful and appreciative towards all. You should not be attached to your past, as this is *uppekha*. And always learn to forgive. When you feel that these qualities have developed inside you, spread them out towards all directions in the world after every dhyana.' The Buddha fell silent after his long address.

In the evening, Tathagata related to his *sangha*, 'The bad *kamma* of the Sakyas and Mahanama is bound to lead them to more sufferings. Bad *kamma*s of both Mahanama and Pasenadi led to the death of Vasabhakhatiya. Vidudabha is lonesome and spiteful due to Mahanama and Pasenadi's actions and for his own bad deeds. The wrongful *kamma*s of Pasenadi, Mahanama, and the Sakyas have converted the simple, innocent, and naive Vidudabha into a cruel person, who is now full of vengeance in his heart. He shall destroy Kapilavatthu and the Sakyas in a few days. This evil *kamma* will, in turn, furnish an ill outcome, and Kosala shall not recover from it.' The *sangha* listened to Tathagata's prophetic assertion with much trepidation.

BOOK II

Digha Karayana
(Commander of Kosala Army)

To live in the world with your heart undisturbed by the world, with all sorrows ended, dwelling in peace—this is the greatest happiness.

—Mangala Sutta

I, Digha Karayana, am the commander-in-chief of the Kosala army today. I, however, was appointed as a mere soldier in the Kosala army during the time of Maharaja Mahakosala, and was soon elevated to the rank of the senapati. Since then, I have served my country with all my heart and soul. I have fought several battles for my land and seldom suffered defeat. Everybody knows me as a vicious, merciless, and a hard-hitting warrior. My various techniques of war are revered even by the bitterest of my enemies. That, lately, I have converted to the *dhamma* of the Buddha is barely known to many. Keeping in constant touch with the *sangha*, I often visit Tathagata to listen to his sacred discourses. During the rains, when the Buddha usually visits Jethavan, I scarcely fail to attend his sermons.

An orphan, I was raised by my maternal uncle Bandhula in Kusinara. When he and his children were killed by Maharaja Pasenadi at the instigation of the corrupt officials of Savathi, my wrath knew no bounds. Since then, I have been trying my best to avenge their deaths when I found my dice in Vidudabha. I could perceive the trauma and suffering that Yuvraj Vidudabha and his mother Rani Vasabhakhatiya was going through. I had known the prince since he was a sweet little boy. He would play on my shoulders and, many a time, I would be his horse and he would sit on me posing as the Maharaja of Kosala. Mahanama's malevolent conspiracy and his callous abuses on him, as well as his father Maharaja Pasenadi's ordeals on the young prince and on his queen mother transformed the benevolent and the merry prince into an irate and a glum one.

Vidudabha and I were both victims of Pasenadi's spite. Therefore, to teach the king a lesson, I wanted Kumar by my side. My intent was simple and unambiguous—to overthrow Pasenadi and establish Vidudabha as the Maharaja of Kosala.

***

Vidudabha, subsequent to his enthronement, received offerings and greetings from various kingdoms and *ganarajyas* across the land. Though the younger generation in Kosala were in high spirits at the crowning of the young prince Vidudabha, the older folks were dissatisfied at the manner in which Pasenadi was dethroned. However, my standing instructions to the military and the snoopers were to deal with such intimidating people with austerity and, if need be, even exterminated. Very soon, peace returned to Savathi and Kosala. In due course of time, Vidudabha became a very efficient administrator. Corrupt officials were dealt with harshness, and the poor and the needy with sympathy. Taxes were simplified and, wherever required, even reduced, leading to a boom in business and agriculture. Artisans and their handicrafts received much boost. Soldiers stationed at regular intervals on highways checked the pillaging of traders and the common men by highway brigands. Surveys were conducted for irrigation canals to reroute water from the mighty Achiravati for the benefit of the farmers. The construction of roads to connect the interior villages to Savathi and other major towns of the *mahajanapada* began. Kosala was gradually becoming a happy place to live in, and Vidudabha steadily built a niche in every Kosala's heart.

In the palace, Vidudabha had anointed the former Maharani Mallika as the queen mother of the state, and her seat was positioned next to his. But I had entirely forgotten that beneath the composed mien of Maharaja Vidudabha, the inferno of the unfulfilled vow of vengeance seethed.

Hatred is never appeased by hatred in this world. By non-hatred alone is hatred appeased. This is a law eternal.

—Dhammapada

'Senapati,' the king sent for me one afternoon. 'Time has finally arrived for us to honour my oath that I took as a young boy.'

'Maharaj, I fail to remember what that is,' I replied.

'This is surprising, Senapati, that you could forget such a thing,' Vidudabha expressed dismay and then continued, 'Do you not remember my pitiless childhood because of Mahanama and the Sakyas? Have you forgotten how my mother died due to Mahanama and my father's misdeeds? The brutal insults and the profanities of my grandfather and the Sakyas of which I was a victim? All those brutalities made me pledge to slay Mahanama and wipe out Kapilavatthu.' Vidudabha's reminder suddenly flooded me with pathetic and harsh memories of his adolescent days in Kapilavatthu. His vow to decimate the entire Sakya clan, including Mahanama, who were instrumental in his mother's and his own endless woes came to my mind.

'Your Highness, have we not had enough bloodshed?' I reminded him of the carnage that had occurred in the process of his coronation.

'Yes, we did, Senapati. But my oath still remains to be fulfilled. Does it not?' asked Vidudabha, looking straight into my eyes.

'I know Maharaj, the sufferings you and your Queen Mother had undergone are difficult for you to forget, but to grant them forgiveness is the greatest merit,' I pleaded to the king. A follower of the Buddha's *dhamma*, I tried to prevent the king from massacring the Sakyas to satiate his thirst for revenge, which I now knew would be his bad *kamma*, resulting in a dreadful consequence.

While converting to the Buddha's *dhamma*, I believed that each grass and insect, each tree and bird, and each animal of the land had accepted Buddha's compassion and harmony, which he was preaching among the humans far and wide. Knowing that Maharaja Vidudabha had always been a generous and a compassionate person, I hoped that he too may have been swept by the wave of love and kindness enthused by the Buddha. I expected him to confer mercy on Mahanama and the Sakyas.

'Maharaj, should you not leave Mahanama and the Sakyas to their own *kamma*? They would undeniably face *dukkha* for their abysmal deeds. Did you not see how your father, the great Pasenadi, died a pitiless death as a consequence of his own *kammas*?'

'Digha, you talk of love and forgiveness for Mahanama and his Sakyas, but these words mean nothing to me now. Was it not due to my father and grandfather that my adolescence was wasted? Was it not because of them that my mother died a painful death? And you, my dearest Digha, you expect my clemency for them? All these years, I have kept the flames of revenge blazing within me. Not even for a single moment have I attempted to extinguish it. Yes, I too need peace within me; that, however, would come to me only after the decimation of Mahanama and Kapilavatthu. My dear Senapati, only their end can bring solace to the wounded soul of my deceased mother and that of mine.'

I could see how unbending Vidudabha was, which, of course, was quite comprehensible on his part. I knew that no reasoning could impede him from destroying Mahanama and Kapilavatthu.

'Senapati,' Maharaja Vidudabha called for me the following day. 'Prepare your army for the attack on Kapilavatthu. I shall notify you about the day of the assault.'

'Yes, Your Honour,' I responded softly.

Another workaday evening. The setting sun was still veiled by the grey clouds, when I spotted Maharaja Vidudabha ride with his guards in the distance. I knew then that he was heading towards his mother's *thuppa*, possibly to seek her blessings for his oncoming assault on Kapilavatthu. If that be the case, then we were to set off for the attack in a few days' time. As conjectured, I was summoned by the king in the night.

'Senapati, we will set out to besiege Kapilavatthu in two days.'

'Yes, My Lord,' I replied in submission.

'We reach there in three days. You know what we are to do there. Not a single Sakya is to remain alive,' Vidudabha looked in to my eyes. 'Mahanama should not be spared. Senapati, now go and prepare your army for the attack.' Commanding thus, the king slowly retreated to his chamber.

It was night-time and I was the only one left in the large assembly after the king had departed. A cold shiver ran through me. I had fought several battles, but never one where my army were to slaughter infants, children, and women, disabled, ailing, and the elderly. I ruminated on how Kumar, who once was so sympathetic and considerate towards all, could suddenly become so cold-blooded and spiteful.

He who can curb his wrath as soon as it arises, as a timely antidote will check snake's venom that so quickly spreads.

—Sutta Nipata

It had rained night-long. Though the downpour had stopped now, the morning sky was still enveloped with dark gloomy clouds. The large contingent of our Kosala army stood on the ground beside the palace, ready to ride, while the citizens gathered near the palace in large numbers to bid us farewell. Eventually, Maharaja Vidudabha joined us. He sat on a well-ornamented royal elephant with me by his side on a *ratha* and we set off for Kapilavatthu.

No sooner did we ride for about a twenty *kosas* from Savathi than we spotted an orange-robed old monk in the distance meditating under a dead tree. Moving closer, we discovered that he was none other than the Buddha himself. His presence there astonished us.

That Vidudabha would be travelling to Kapilavatthu to decimate the city and annihilate its people was known to the Sakyamuni. It appeared that it was apparent to him that the Sakyas and Mahanama were fated to suffer the consequences of their wrong *kamma* at the hands of Maharaja Vidudabha.

Conscious of the established norm that an army would abort its mission to attack and return if they spot an ascetic on its way, Tathagata deliberately sat meditating by the highway through which the Kosala army was to proceed to Kapilavatthu. Sighting The Venerated One, Vidudabha raised his hands, signalling his army to stop. The king, unlike his father, wasn't an adherent of the *dhamma* of the Buddha, but he revered him intensely as it was for him that both he and his mother were redeemed from slavery.

'Senapati, since the Sakyamuni sits under that tree by the road to Kapilavatthu, it becomes an impediment to our assignment. We should return to Savathi this time. We shall have to venture to Kapilavatthu some other day,' advised Vidudabha.

'Yes, Maharaj, that would be the correct thing to do. Besides, Maharaj Pasenadi was Buddha's ardent follower and Maharani Mai still venerates him devotedly.' I commanded the army to turn back.

***

We embarked on our journey to Kapilavatthu a few days later only to find the Buddha seated in the meditative posture under the same tree again. I understood that The Enlightened One was doing this on purpose to prevent the carnage in Kapilavatthu from happening, and, in the process, was protecting Vidudabha from committing a heinous crime and bad *kamma*, which would be the cause of his sufferings consequently. But we were indeed astonished as to how the Buddha knew that we would be journeying that very day.

We returned to Savathi again, that very instant.

***

A few days later, we set out for Kapilavatthu once again. But this time we took a different way, a deserted highway that was abandoned both by travellers and tradesmen as they found the road unfit to travel due to its ruggedness.

'Senapati, since this is a longer road to Kapilavatthu, ask your men to hasten,' the king ordered.

Barely did we ride a few *kosas* from Savathi than in the distance we spotted the Buddha once again in his saffron robe, meditating under another dead tree by the road to Kapilavatthu.

'That is Tathagata again!' exclaimed the king.

'How on earth did he come here?' Even I was in for a surprise. 'How did he know that we were to pass through this road?'

Vidudabha alighted from his elephant and advanced towards the Buddha. I too followed the king. We kissed his sacred feet.

'O Master, why do we always find you meditating under dead trees? Should you not be doing your dhyana under green and shaded trees, where, at your age, you would find the most comfort?' Vidudabha asked the Buddha with folded hands.

'Maharaj, my own people provide me the most comforting shade,' replied the Buddha. I marked the words that The Enlightened One voiced—'*my own people*'. I believed that he was referring to the Sakyas, his own people, whom he desired to shield from Vidudabha's wrath. I presumed that the king too understood what Tathagata meant, as I saw his face colour on hearing the Buddha's rejoinder.

'Maharaj Vidudabha,' said The Enlightened One as we were preparing to return. 'May you look at this world with kindness, forgiveness, and gratitude. I wish you all happiness and compassion. I pray that no harm is wished on another by anger or hatred, and no one hates or despises the other. I plead you to let go of your past.'

As we rode back to Savathi, I felt that Tathagata's words had no effect on Vidudabha as he remained silent in suppressed anger.

'Senapati, tomorrow we shall ride to Kapilavatthu by our earlier path. No one, not even the presence of the Buddha, should stop us,' the king spoke firmly.

The following morning, as we rode through the previous highway, the revered Buddha could not be located anywhere. The barren tree stood at the same place. I bowed to it all the same with deep reverence, as the Buddha's *vipassana* under it had made the tree and its shade holy. Although he wasn't there today, I knew that he did make a few attempts to avert the massacre by stopping us from travelling to Kapilavatthu.

But Maharaja Vidudabha's perseverance was evidently perceptible. I realized that nothing now could thwart us from heading for Kapilavatthu, not even the holy presence of the Buddha who, mercifully, wasn't anywhere to be seen.

Just as with her own life, a mother shields from hurt her own son, her only child, let all-embracing thoughts for all beings be yours.

—**Metta Sutta**

The snow-capped mountains of the majestic Himalayas in the horizon gleamed pink in the glare of the rising sun. The graceful Rohini River, which flowed at a distance, demarcated the territories of the Sakyas and the Koliyas. The walled boundary of Kapilavatthu gradually came closer to us as we rode towards it on the third morning of our journey. The gates of the city that were opened till now slowly closed down. Perhaps, they had sighted us. The arrival of our large army must have evoked panic in their hearts. The Sakyas, I knew, stood no chance against the mighty Kosala army.

'Break in! Do not give Mahanama and the Sakyas a chance to resist our attack. We should catch them by surprise. Surround the city and break in through all the gates. We enter and begin the carnage. Spare no one! Kill them all—women, children, and the aged. Let no one escape,' ordered Maharaja Vidudabha.

I commanded my soldiers, 'Enclose the city and break in through the gates. A-T-T-A-C-K!'

As we were about to force our way in, the main gate of Kapilavatthu opened, allowing us to enter without any resistance. A bit surprised, we led our soldiers inside the city through the gate. We were stopped on our way by Bhalatiya and Harita, the two councillors of the *mahajanapada* of Kapilavatthu, with a large troop of soldiers.

'*Johar*, Maharaj Vidudabha of Kosala. Welcome to the land of your mother,' both the *amalas* greeted the king.

'Senapati,' Vidudabha looked at me and asked me with a smile. 'Remember these two oafs?'

'How can I forget them, Your Highness? They had laughed and scoffed and even spat on seeing you in their *santhagara* when you had come here in your younger days. And today they approach you with respect and humility. How they change colours like chameleons!' I replied.

'How right you are, Senapati,' replied the king. 'Where are your contemptuous smiles, you filthy Sakyas? Now when death stands in front of you, you act so humbly towards me. Where was your humbleness when I was young? And you louts think that your soldiers can stop us?' Vidudabha thundered at them. He looked at me to give the signal to kill the soldiers. I ordered my men to clash with the Sakya army. They charged at the enemy and, in no time, most of the Sakya soldiers lay dead on the ground, while the rest ran off. I found both the councillors shuddering.

'Mahout, instruct your elephant to crush these two Sakyas to death!' bellowed Maharaja Vidudabha.

'Mercy, O Great King, have mercy on us,' both the councillors fell on the ground, begging forgiveness. The elephant was already commanded, and in no time it crushed their heads like pulp. Blood gushed out, drenching the dry earth. Seeing the horrendous spectacle, a pandemonium spread among the nearby people who scampered away howling in fright.

I prayed to the Buddha silently to forgive my sin of killing the innocents. Suddenly, we noticed a sandstorm approaching us through the streets of the city, which we knew was the Sakya army speeding towards us.

'ATTACK!' I ordered my army. The soldiers dashed, letting out dreadful cries that curled the blood of everyone. As we were about to thrust ahead, we were abruptly drawn to a halt. Someone stood in our way.

It was Mahanama flanked by a group of councillors, who stood right across us.

'S-T-O-P!' the king shouted vociferously, raising his right hand and signalling the army to come to a standstill. Mahanama, who seemed to retain the same arrogance he once possessed, stood glaring at Vidudabha. The councillors had already gestured their advancing army to halt.

'Mahanayaka or Raja, whoever you are, your slave grandson has returned,' Vidudabha mocked, sitting on his elephant and looking down at Mahanama.

'I can see that,' Mahanama remarked in vanity.

'My dear Mahanama, do you remember the first time when I had come to learn archery from you, how you and your people behaved with me, as if I was some sort of a pariah dog and not a human? Do you?'

Even I was stunned to hear the king call his grandfather by his name.

Mahanama did not reply.

'I asked you a question, old fellow. Do you remember or do you not?' roared Vidudabha.

'Ye-ye-yes, I do,' stammered Mahanama.

'Good,' Vidudabha gestured his mahout to let his elephant kneel down so that he could alight. Once on the ground, Vidudabha walked up to Mahanama and, looking straight into his eyes, remarked tenderly yet assertively, 'Now, old chap, I want you to tell your *amala*s standing behind you to kiss my feet.

Now!' Hearing this, Mahanama and the councillors looked very edgy and hesitant.

'Right now!' roared the king. Every councillor, except Mahanama, hastened to kiss his feet. Vidudabha then silently gestured his soldiers, who, wasting no time, came and chopped off their heads. Mahanama stood bewildered in shock. The Sakya army instantly charged towards us.

'C-H-A-R-G-E!' I screamed at my soldiers.

The confontration began, and we fought for long. Although quite a few of our men were martyred, we eventually defeated the Sakyas and killed them all.

'Mahanama,' roared Vidudabha, 'this is so very agonizing, you know. But then, who but you can be blamed for all this? You wronged by tricking my father. You are the reason that my father hated my mother and me, and it was for you that my mother suffered all through her life and died. You are responsible for ruining my childhood.' The maharaja of Kosala slowly circumambulated Mahanama as he condemned him. He suddenly stopped and asked, 'Where is my grandmother Nagamunda?'

'She is dead.'

'What!' Vidudabha was shocked. 'So, Mahanama, you killed the unfortunate woman too?'

'No, I did not kill her. She died a natural death.'

'She may have died on her own, but she must have died in deep anguish on hearing about her only daughter's grievous death in Savathi, which was the outcome of your appalling actions.'

The raja had no answer to Vidudabha's accusations.

'Well, you are to be punished. You and your people for all the wrongs you committed on me, my mother, and on my grandmother,' Vidudabha's face hardened.

'Senapati,' Vidudabha turned towards me. 'Order your men to kill each and every Sakya. Show no pity to anyone.'

'O Maharaj, have mercy,' pleaded Mahanama quite unexpectedly, clasping his wrinkled and trembling hands. 'I know that I have committed much offence against you and your parents. Your anger is just. But that I am your grandfather cannot be rebuffed, can it? As your grandfather, can I make a request? To keep it or not is up to you.'

'Speak,' commanded Vidudabha.

'You are my grandson, and in you runs my blood; that cannot be denied. On the basis of this relationship, which I have not been able to honour, I beg of you to refrain from slaughtering the innocent citizens who are in no way connected with the anguish in your life. Can I acquaint you with a plan that I have just thought of?' Mahanama requested with folded hands. Vidudabha nodded with conceit, without uttering any word.

The raja resumed after remaining silent for a while, 'Maharaj Vidudabha, permit me to immerse myself in the water of our sacred tank. Till I emerge from the water, I plead to you to let my innocent people flee Kapilavatthu. After I rise from the water, you can kill me and the remaining Sakyas. That is all I seek.'

Vidudabha seemed to be in a fix. He smiled looking at me.

'Senapati,' said Maharaja Vidudabha. 'What do you think of this proposition of the Nayaka?'

'Tricky situation, Sire,' I replied. 'But then, how many people can escape in the duration of a man submerged in water? I do not think he can hold his breath for long inside water.'

'You are right. I guess we can give our consent to his suggestion,' Vidudabha smiled. Then, turning towards Mahanama, he declared, 'Alright, old man, you may proceed.'

'My grandson,' said the nayaka of Kapilavatthu, keeping his hands clasped. 'In case I do not surface out of the water and die inside, forgive me, if possible, for the plight you have been subjected to for the evils committed by me.'

Mahanama went down the steps of the sacred ghat of the tank. He paused for a while to shed his cloak, and then continued descending into the pond. Bit by bit, he sank slowly into the depths of the water till a portion of his bald head was the final thing that was seen on the surface of the water. Then, nothing was visible except ripples in the water.

In whom there is no sympathy for living beings, know him as an outcast.

—Sutta Nipata

The submergence of Mahanama in the tank gave time to a large number of people of Kapilavatthu to escape with their belongings; some carrying them on their heads, some under their arms, while some even dragged them. Women hauled their children and their cattle, while many even heaved their elders. Bullock carts in hundreds hurried along the road outside the city. Clouds of dust shrouded the city streets while the dogs barked.

As the people fled, we waited for the old raja to surface from the tank. 'This is taking quite long, Senapati. How can a man stay in the water for so long?' Vidudabha's voice displayed concern.

'Alright, Your Highness, let me send a few soldiers inside the pond to check,' I answered the king. Two of my soldiers, who were good swimmers, plunged into the pond to look for old Mahanama.

They scoured in the water scrupulously. 'He is not here,' one of the soldiers yelled from the side of the pond where Mahanama had drowned himself. Both scanned the tank once more and finally hollered, 'We have found him ... he is at *this* side of the pond, dead!' They both dragged the corpse of the old nayaka to the ghat.

'He had tied himself to a large boulder underwater,' the other soldier said. I tried to introspect what Mahanama's plan was.

'Maharaj,' I revealed to Vidudabha. 'Mahanama may have immersed on this side of the pond, but he swam to the other side. Being well-versed in yoga, he was able to hold his breath long enough to tie a large stone and keep himself submerged and eventually die. The entire process, though brief, gave ample time to a large number of his people to escape.'

'Oh,' Vidudabha moaned. 'What a clever deceiver this old fox was! He cheated my parents and now he tricked us again to escape death from my hands and also let hundreds of Sakyas run away.'

'Let not a Sakya live! Even the ones who have run away couldn't have gone far. Kill them all!' Vidudabha turned towards me and screamed in rage. Soon the sky was filled with screams and howls of men, women, and children. I wondered why there wasn't any resistance from the Sakyas. Where was the rest of their army?

By afternoon, the bloodbath was over. The soil, wherever visible, was drenched in red. Death was everywhere. Corpses, with or without heads or limbs, lay scattered like straw on the soil, while the half-dead moaned in severe pain. Several infants had embraced death in the laps of their mothers. You couldn't walk or ride your horse without stumbling on a dead Sakya. The water of a pond, a little far from the city where loads of dead bodies were dumped, had turned red. The wind stopped blowing as evening was gradually setting in. Vultures gyrated above us, and foxes and hyenas sneaked in on sniffing the reek of blood and dead flesh. Seeing Tathagata's own people die in this manner was indeed excruciating.

Darkness was slowly setting in when I saw Maharaja Vidudabha emerge indolently from a small lane in Kapilavatthu. Was he finally happy and content now that his vengeance was met? I could not say. In the fading light of the dusk, I found his face grim and stiffened by stress. Whether this was satisfaction or remorse, I could not distinguish.

Coming to me, he slowly but solemnly commanded, 'Let us return. We are done here.'

BOOK III

After the Bloodbath ...

Why do what you will regret? Why bring tears upon yourself?
Do only what you do not regret, and fill yourself with joy.

—Dhammapada

Tathagata and his disciples were sitting by a lake at Mahavan in Veshali when the news of the carnage of Kapilavatthu reached him. Hearing this, Ananda, one of the favourite disciples of Siddhartha and a Sakya himself, could not withhold his tears.

'Is this not an immeasurable tragedy, O Master?' asked Ananda.

Siddhartha had triumphed over the senses of pain and pleasure. Nevertheless, today he did very well perceive the anguish of the massacre of such a large sea of humanity, who were his own people. This colossal calamity was an event not seen or heard by anyone before. However, Tathagata had attempted to prevent the disaster earlier as he foresaw the approaching catastrophe.

'Why do you weep, Ananda? I believe that you lament the deaths of your near and dear ones in Kapilavatthu,' Buddha, on finding Ananda in tears, beckoned him to come closer. 'It seems that you haven't yet conquered your attachments. Attachment, as you already know, is the source of all sorrows. Haven't I told you never to fight your sorrow but let it die its own death? Do you not meditate to free yourself from all the attachments that bind you to this material world? So do it, *Bhantey*, as only then would you get rid of your attachments.'

'Yes, Master,' replied Ananda.

In the evening, the sun set behind the hills in the forest of Mahavan. The fading soft colours of the twilight sky looked beautiful and a tender breeze blew, bringing the *bhikkhus* respite from the heat. Sitting by the lake, the Buddha sermonized to his *sangha*.

'The carnage of the Sakyas is indeed a heart-rending event, for they paid heavily for the wrong *kamma* of Mahanama and his councillors. Now Vidudabha will face the consequence for his bad *kamma* against Kapilavatthu,' the Buddha speaking thus, closed his eyes in dhyana.

Next afternoon, after they returned from their *pindapata*, the Buddha and his *sangha* rested under a tree beside the lake. The walk was exasperating for the Buddha due to his old age. Kassapa brought some water in a leaf *dona* for The Enlightened One, who drank to his heart's content and then looked up at him.

'All these years, I have been preaching the *dhamma* of compassion and peace,' said the Buddha. 'I have preached the *dhamma* to Maharaj Pasenadi, Maharani Mallika, Maharaj Bimbisara, Nayaka Bandhula, the villainous Angulimal, and to the entire kingdom. Although they tell me that the birds in the sky and the trees on the ground where I roam talk of love and compassion, I could not curb the hatred and violence that sprouted in Vidudabha. My discourse of love could not win over the hatred in him. I failed to prevent the carnage of my very own people, the Sakyas, and neither could avert the complete destruction of Kapilavatthu.

'It seems that people have not fully understood the *dhamma* that I am preaching. They are still attached to material desires and do not seek deliverance from *dukkha*. They may have adopted the *dhamma*, but only to seek change from the existing circumstances; therefore, I am afraid that once I am gone, which will be very soon, the places where I have sermonized on peace, love, and compassion will be plagued with conflict and war,' Tathagata said and shut his eyes to meditate.

He who inflicts violence on those who are unarmed, and offends those who are inoffensive, will soon come upon one of these ten states: sharp pain, or disaster, bodily injury, serious illness, or derangement of mind, trouble from the government, or grave charges, loss of relatives, or loss of wealth, or houses destroyed by ravaging fire; upon dissolution of the body that ignorant man is born in hell.

—Dhammapada

Vidudabha eventually reached Savathi with his victorious army. Dismounting his elephant, he walked slowly to the palace. The maharaja's strides, as Digha observed, were devoid of any zeal or jollity. Since his return from Kapilavatthu, the king had not uttered a word. Was he in remorse then, the senapati wondered. The triumph of the Kosala army brought cheer in the palace and in the city. Celebrations began, but Vidudabha was nowhere to be seen. In the evening, when the amusement in the palace was at its peak, the king quietly slipped out and rode to the mound of his mother. As the waning hues of the dusk were setting in, Vidudabha languidly treaded towards his mother's *thuppa* with the wind playing softly with his hair.

Falling on the mound, he dug his face into the soil of the monument and embraced it as if the *thuppa* was a personification of his mother. Then he started weeping.

'Mai,' the king sobbed like a child in confession. 'I have avenged your death and my insults by killing them all—infants, handicapped, the old, women, even pregnant ones, and also compelled your father Mahanama to die. Mahanama, who tormented you all your life and for whom you died so early, leaving me alone in this heartless world. But Mai, why is there no solace in me? Why? My heart burns, my whole body aches, and sleep has evaded me. Oh, what have I done, Mai? What have I done?'

***

The court was adjourned the following day as the king refused to come out of his room. He hadn't eaten anything since the previous day. Maharaja Vidudabha's strange behaviour became a matter of intense concern both in the palace and in Savathi. As a consequence, victory celebrations were suddenly halted. Gossips spread widely. People discussed among themselves whether such a bloodbath in Kapilavatthu brought about a change in Vidudabha's heart, or was he repenting for his heinous deed?

Digha, the king's closest friend, philosopher, and guide was summoned by Maharaja Vidudabha in the afternoon. He hastened into the king's room and the doors slammed behind him. About an hour later, the senapati emerged from the maharaja's chamber wearing a pensive expression on his face. He did not utter a single word to anyone.

Late in the evening, deafening screams suddenly resonated in the palace, 'Fire, fire!' Sentries and officials and the queen mother all rushed towards the king's quarter, which was engulfed in flames. Servants sprayed tubs of water to douse the intensifying blaze, but the fire was too huge for them to put out. The royal room with Vidudabha, the maharaja of Kosala, was razed to ashes.

'O, what a disaster! The Maharaj has burnt to death! Who shall be the next king? What will happen to Kosala?'

Only Digha Karayana, the senapati of Kosala and the king's loyal friend, stood in the distance with tears relentlessly rolling down his cheeks. He knew the reason behind the fire outbreak and the maharaja's death.

'May you finally get your peace, love, and respect, my king! The things you were deprived of all your life, may you obtain them in the arms of death. Farewell, my dear friend, Vidudabha. Farewell forever.'

EPILOGUE

With Kapilavatthu devastated, his people terminated, his only son Rahula dead, and age taking the better of him, Buddha appeared wrecked. But he was The Awakened One who had risen above all the earthly pleasures and pains, and worldly happiness and misery as such had no effect on him.

Eliminating the guru–shishya tradition, and trusting his own formulated ideology *appo dipa bhava* (be thy own light), Siddhartha had acquired enlightenment and transformed into the Buddha so that he could dedicate his life enlightening people and guide them towards cessation from their *dukkha* in this *samsara*.

Arriving in Kusinagara, the capital city of the Mallas, the Sakyamuni was struck down with food poisoning and, eventually, in a sacred grove of sal trees, he breathed his last among his disciples. With his death, he left behind his *dhamma* of the Middle Path and the teachings of the Noble Eightfold Path, non-attachment, love, brotherhood, and compassion for his disciples to spread it among the sufferers in the world.

The sacred body of the Buddha was kept in a sarcophagus and cremated on the seventh day of his *mahaparinibbana* by the Mallas of Kusinagara. The seven clans waged a war against the Mallas who desired to keep the relics of the Buddha to themselves, as they felt that it was in their land that The Enlightened One had acquired *mahaparinibbana*. However, the Mallas gave in after the battle and the sacred relics were subsequently divided into eight vessels and distributed among Ajatsattu of Magadha, the Mallas of Kusinagara and of Pava, the Bulis of Allakappa, the Koliyas of Ramagrama, the Licchavis of Veshali, and a Brahmin of Vethadipa, while the final vessel of the Sakyamuni's relics was acquired by a few of the remaining Sakyas.

It is believed that not all Sakyas had died in the bloodshed unleashed by Maharaja Vidudabha. Although the *ganarajya* of the Sakyas was destroyed in the carnage, a few Sakyas did survive, many of who were assumed to have escaped to Nepal. Some others had fled to the country of the Koliyas and a few to Pipphalivana.

After the death of Vidudabha, the *mahajanapada* of Kosala collapsed. Maharaja Ajatsattu declared war on Veshali and subsequently took possession of it. He later annexed Kashi and Kosala to Magadha, thereby ending the lineage of the great King Mahakosala.

GLOSSARY

aarti: sacred light from a flame offered to a deity or to a person of a high status

abhayadan: a posture of Buddha's hands offering reassurance from fear

acelas: ascetics of ancient India belonging to the Ajivika or Jaina sect

akhada: a wrestling ring

amartyas/amalas: councillors

bhaktin: a non-Brahmin female priest

bhandar: store

bhantey: a term to refer Buddhists monks in the Theravada tradition

bhikkhu/bhikunni (*bhikhshu/bhikhshuni* in Sanskrit): literally meaning beggars, *bhikkhu*/bhikunni are Pali words for Buddhist monks and nuns who survive on alms

bhojpatra: bark of the birch tree that grows in the Himalayas, which were used as writing paper in ancient India

chowki: a seat/bed made of wood

chua-chui: a popular game among children in India, also known as *tag*, *tiggy*, etc.

dafali: tambourine

dasa: male slave

dasi: female slave

dhals: shields used in war by soldiers

dhamma: the truth taught by the Buddha that leads to the awakening of a seeker

dhibri: a lamp used in ancient India, still found in villages

dona: a small container made from leaves of sal trees

dukkha: sorrow

ekadasi: eleventh lunar day of the waxing phases of the moon

gachti: a pledge of an offering to a deity if one's wish is fulfilled (assumed to be by the deity) *ganarajya/ganasangha*: refers to a type of republic

homa: Vedic fire ritual, also known as yagna

johar: a non-Sanskrit greeting once popular in India; today *johar* is restrained to the tribals and dalits in East and West India

Jyeshtha: a month in the various Hindu calendars that falls in the Gregorian calendarical months of May or June

kamma (karma in Sanskrit): Pali term for 'deed' or 'action'

kavirajas: upper-caste practitioners of Ayurvedic medicine

kosa (krosa in Sanskrit): measurement of distance in ancient India

kushti: wrestling

madaris: street performers of magic and other entertaining plays

maggo (*marga* in Sanskrit): Pali term for path referring to the Eightfold Path of the Buddha

mahaparinibbana: Pali word for the ultimate state of nirvana, where an awakened being attains eternal bliss

mai: mother

Mundas: a Proto-Australoid tribe that speaks the Austric Mundari language; they are believed to have entered India in the second millennium BCE. Mundari is supposedly one of the oldest languages that was once widely spoken in prehistoric India

naresh: king

nibbana (nirvana in Sanskrit): a Pali word that implies the final 'blow out' or the ultimate liberation from rebirth and is the final goal of humans according to the Theravada tradition

parishadkuti: office of the council

phonta: a sacred mark worn on the forehead

pindapata: alms round or 'lump dropping'; the monastics survive on alms acquired from *pindapata*

pothi: writings on palm leaves or birch barks that were used as pages and were tied together to give it a form of a book

rajjyotishi: royal astrologer

rajvaidya: an ayurvedic medicine practitioner of a royal family *ratha*: chariot

samana (*shramana* in Sanskrit): non-Brahmanical ascetics like Buddhists, Jainas, Charvakas, Ajivikas, and others

samsara: The world where one is locked in the cycle of re-births and deaths

sangha: monastic community of *bhikshus* (monks) and *bhikshunis* (nuns)

santhagara: assembly hall of the Sakya council

sarai: a resting place for travellers

sarna: sacred groves of the Mundari and other tribes; such groves ideally comprise at least five sacred sal trees

semul: a tree in India in which cotton is grown and beautiful red flowers bloom on it during spring

shradhya: a funerary ritual performed by the closest relative of the departed to pay homage to the deceased; the ceremony is conducted by a Brahman priest

Sin Bonga: one of the major deities worshipped by the Mundaris and several other tribes since the prehistoric period

sonar: goldsmith

thaila: satchel

thuppa (stupa in Sanskrit): hemispherical architecture containing relics of the dead

totka: indigenous remedies

vaidya: ayurvedic medicine practitioner

vanna: Pali word of the Sanskrit term 'varna'

Vesak: Pali word for the month of Vaishakh that falls in April/May of the Gregorian calendar

vyakhyana/vitarka: a posture of Buddha's fingers during his preaching or instruction

yavan: refers to Greeks or any foreigners in ancient Indian texts

ACKNOWLEDGEMENTS

My earnest gratitude is for Mr Bikash Niyogi and Mrs Tultul Niyogi for consenting to publish the manuscript. My thanks to Mr Nirmal Kanti Bhattacharjee of Niyogi Books for finding this manuscript enthralling and absorbing and to Ms Sukanya Sur for thoroughly and scrupulously editing the entire manuscript.

My heartfelt thanks to Mr Shashi Bhushan Prasad for painstakingly laying out the book and to Kaushikee for tastefully designing the cover of the book.

Born in Dibrugarh, Assam in 1956, Subhashis Das is an eminent researcher, educationist, and author of the ancient history of the tribals and their various megaliths. He is also credited with discovering numerous ancient megalithic sites across India, many of which are his study sites. He has authored four books, including *Unknown Civilization of Prehistoric India* (2014) and *The Archaeoastronomy of a Few Megalithic Sites of Jharkhand* (2018), besides writing several papers for many significant journals.

Jharkhand Educational Council has incorporated his discovery and research on megaliths in the history books of the state. National Geographic and Doordarshan have made several documentaries on his discoveries. He often lectures on his researches and discoveries on megaliths and tribalism across the country and abroad.